The
Sleuth's Conundrum

The
Sleuth's Conundrum

The Librarian Sleuth—Book Three

By
Kimberly Rose Johnson

Dedication

This book is dedicated to librarians everywhere. Thank you for making sure we have great books to read!

Acknowledgments

Special thanks to everyone who had a hand in making this book what it is. I am grateful for the passion you put into making this book the best it could be.

Maybe I shouldn't admit this, but this was one of the most difficult books I've ever written. I am forever grateful to Angela Ruth Strong for helping me when I was so stuck, I couldn't move forward.

Chapter One

TARA JAMES WAVED TO ONE OF the sheriff deputies as he stopped his car for her to cross. She raced across the street as the dark clouds overhead released a deluge of water—fitting, considering how her morning had started. Rain dripped from her raincoat hood onto her face. Why today of all days did her car have to die? At least it wasn't foggy here like it had been at her house. Lightening flashed. She yelped and dashed under the cover of the library awning.

A soft cry caught her attention. She looked to her right and then left and gasped. "What are you doing there all alone?" A tiny baby lay wrapped in a pink blanket, cradled in a baby carrier.

She checked to see if anyone was nearby. Who would leave a newborn outside and all alone, especially in a storm like this? No one walked or loitered nearby. Tara frowned and grasped the handle of the baby carrier tucked behind a large flowerpot. She grunted at the weight. "My you're a heavy little girl for being so small," Tara cooed as she reached for the diaper bag sitting behind it. "Hello, precious. We need to get you inside where it's warm and dry."

Why weren't the doors opening? She stood in the trigger zone. "Wait a minute." The entire library was blanketed in darkness—the power must be out. Surely Nancy was inside though. She reached for the little-used door to the right of the sliding door and tugged. It didn't budge. The infant's cries increased in intensity. "Shh, little one." Now what should she do? She never remembered to carry an umbrella, and the baby would get soaked if they left the cover of the awning.

The doors suddenly slid open, and the lights turned on. "It's your lucky day," Tara said. The irony of her comment was not lost on her.

Nancy, her boss and the head librarian, greeted her from behind the circulation or check-out desk, as Tara preferred to call it. "Who do you have there?"

"I'm not sure. She was sitting outside the library all alone."

"She?" Nancy stood and walked around the desk, her boot heels clicking on the blue concrete flooring.

"I assume she, since she has a pink blanket and hat."

"You didn't see anyone that could've been her parent?"

Tara shook her head. "What do we do?" She set the carrier on the floor and shrugged out of her raincoat then hung it on a nearby hook to dry.

"Call the police for starters." Nancy pulled out her phone. "The safe haven law in Oregon makes it legal and easy to drop off a baby up to thirty days old, at a fire or police station, no questions asked. Why would the mother risk jail by not taking her daughter to one of those places?"

"Or a hospital. I've heard about that law, but perhaps her mama hadn't."

The baby cried harder.

Nancy frowned. "Maybe check her diaper. I've only been here an hour, so she wasn't outside all that long." She pulled her long chestnut-colored hair away from her face and used the band on her wrist to create a messy ponytail.

Thunder boomed and rattled the windows. Tara jumped—she hated storms. "I don't remember the last time we had thunder like that." She crossed her arms. "Who would abandon a helpless baby on a day like today?" Tara looked down at the infant and her heart melted. She squatted and unhooked the safety restraint. "How long was the power out?"

"Thirty minutes tops. Are you thinking what I'm thinking?" Nancy moved around her desk and powered on her computer. "I'll pull up the security footage while I get my mom on the phone."

Nancy's mother was the local sheriff, so it made sense that she would call her directly rather than 911. "And I'll see if she needs a diaper change. Do you think she's hungry?"

Nancy shrugged. She had her phone to her ear.

Tara lifted the light-as-a-feather baby from the carrier and cradled her. "Shh. It's going to be okay." The baby quieted and snuggled against her. Her heart melted. Sudden tears burned her eyes. She blinked them away.

Tara knew little about babies, but how hard could changing a diaper be? She peaked inside the diaper bag and spotted an envelope. "What do we have here?" She reached for it then drew out the single sheet of paper.

"This is Amelia. She's a week old. I wish I could keep her but my circumstances won't allow it. Please love her for me and take good care of her." Clearly her mom cared deeply for her so why leave her baby at the library? Amelia started crying again. "Okay, I hear you, precious." Tara dug through the large bag and reached for a changing pad and diaper. "At least your mama left some supplies." She proceeded to change her diaper. Sure enough it was soaked. Poor thing.

Nancy slid her phone into the pocket of her oversized cardigan. "My mom is coming."

"But she's the sheriff. Isn't she more a figure at the department?"

Nancy frowned. "My mom will never be a figurehead. She's as much a cop as the rest of them. Maybe it's not the norm, but that's how it is in Tipton County."

Since she'd been in Tipton, she'd seen the sheriff step outside her job description more than once, so what Nancy said rang true. "Okay, but why not send one of the deputies? There was one out front when I got here. I wonder if he saw anything?"

"I believe her exact words were 'those men wouldn't know the first thing about caring for a baby.' She'd be right too. I don't think any of them have kids. Well, Lyle might, but if he does, they're grown." Nancy came around and peered at the helpless infant. "She likes you."

Tara swaddled the baby in her blanket. "She's sweet when she's not crying."

Nancy grinned. "Was there anything else in her bag?" She squatted and looked inside without touching anything.

"Aren't you going to pull everything out?" Tara lifted Amelia and held her close.

"No. It's evidence."

"Then why didn't you stop me from opening the

envelope?" Honestly, she thought highly of her boss, but at the moment she wasn't pleased—the last thing she needed was her fingerprints all over the evidence.

"I figured the baby's needs were more important." Nancy's face softened. "The two of you look good together." She pulled out her phone. "Let me take your picture with her." She held up her phone. Tara ran a hand through her chin length hair, hoping the storm hadn't made too much of a mess of it. "I'll get one of the two of you then a close up of her."

The library doors slid open and Sheriff Daley strode inside, wearing a long raincoat. "Who do we have here?" She spoke in a soft, gentle voice Tara had never heard the seasoned law-woman use. Babies had a way of bringing out the mushy side of people, and apparently Nancy's mom was no exception.

"This is Amelia. Her mama left a note." Tara handed the slip of paper to the sheriff who now wore a pair of blue gloves.

Nancy looked over her mom's shoulder and took a picture of the note without her knowing.

Sheriff Daley's brow furrowed. "I called the Department of Human Services, but it will be a while before DHS can send someone to take her." She focused on the infant. "How is she?"

"Fine. Other than being cold and wanting to cuddle she seems content now that I've changed her diaper."

The sheriff shook her head. "I will never understand why someone would abandon their child, but to do so outside a library is against the law. Now we have a crime to solve."

Nancy sighed. "What can we do to help?"

"Do either of you know who might have given birth in the last week?"

They both shook their heads.

"I'll check with the local hospital and medical center. Unless the woman was passing through town, I'll find her," the sheriff said.

"Mom, I want to help," Nancy said.

Tara grinned. Her boss had an obsession for solving mysteries. In fact, she seemed happiest when she was on a case. But this was different. A baby's life was put in jeopardy, and now she was parentless. The tragedy of the situation hit Tara. "I'd like to keep Amelia with me."

"That's kind of you," the sheriff said, "but she must be placed with a licensed foster care family."

"How do I become licensed?" Then again, that would be a bad idea, all things considered. If her fingerprints attracted the wrong person's attention...she shuddered.

Nancy's mouth opened slightly. "How would you manage working here and caring for a newborn?"

Tara frowned. "I don't know. How do other mothers do it?"

"They usually have help. I don't know if I could have managed on my own after Nancy was born. She was quite a handful." The sheriff chuckled. "I remember one time—"

"She doesn't need to hear about my childhood antics." Nancy rested a hand at her waist. "What do we do with Amelia until someone from DHS arrives?"

"I'll take her with me."

Tara's heart leapt. "Is that really necessary? She's happy here."

"I'm afraid so, but I won't be leaving for a bit, so enjoy your cuddle time." A soft look covered the sheriff's face before she turned toward her daughter. "I'd like to take a look at the security camera recording."

"I was pulling it up when you arrived. My computer is slow this morning. The storm caused a hard shut off so it's not happy."

"I'll wait." Nancy's mom ran the back of her finger along the baby's cheek. A voice came over her radio, and the sheriff walked outside.

Tara turned to face Nancy. "I feel so bad for this little girl."

"Yeah. It's sad. I wonder what happened that made her mom leave her here. Clearly she loved and cared for Amelia."

The sheriff strode back into the library. "I have to go. Will you girls keep the baby until someone from DHS shows up?"

Nancy nodded. "What's going on?"

"A body was found about a mile outside of town."

Tara gasped. "Murder?"

"We don't know yet. I need to go."

"Well this is shaping up to be quite a morning," Nancy said. "First there's a storm and the power goes out, then a baby shows up, and now we have a possible murder. Talk about a crazy start to the week."

Adam Stacy pulled up behind the sheriff in his white Ford Edge. Rain pounded his windshield and a low roll of thunder added to the cacophony. Had the person been the victim of a hit and run? Someone walking on the side of the road would be nearly impossible to see on a day like today. It made sense considering the weather. Even he'd had a hard time seeing through the heavy rain and had knocked over a trashcan on his way here. Thankfully his SUV hadn't been damaged.

Regardless of the cause of death, he finally had something newsworthy to write about for the Tipton Tribune—this town rarely had anything more exciting to report about than graffiti or a local festival. He tugged on a rain slicker and got out.

"'Morning, Adam," Sheriff Daley said.

"I heard there's a body."

"No comment. You'll need to stay back here."

"Yes, ma'am." He knew the rules, even if he'd never come to the site of a dead body before. He pulled out his camera and zoomed in to see what he couldn't with his naked eye and winced—the top half of the body was covered, but she was wearing a dress and her legs were exposed. A bone poked through the skin on her leg. His stomach roiled, and he turned away after snapping several pictures. He'd seen plenty of dead bodies on television but seeing one in person was a different matter. He took a bracing breath and turned back.

"You'll need to move farther away, Adam." Carter Malone, the town's newest deputy walked toward him. "You look a little green. You feeling okay?"

"Between you and me, I'm not accustomed to seeing a dead body."

"Wish I could say the same."

"That's right, you're from Los Angeles. I imagine

this town is tame compared to where you came from."

"Not as tame as I'd like."

It sounded like the man had a few interesting stories that hadn't come to Adam's attention. Maybe, just maybe, he could get Carter to talk. "What can you tell me about the dead woman?"

Deputy Malone's eyes narrowed. "How'd you know she's female?"

He raised his camera with the telephoto lens he had gifted himself for Christmas last year. "I could see her though this. And I heard it on the scanner, which is how I found out about the accident." *Or murder.*

Carter sighed. "When we know something concrete, the sheriff will make a statement to the press. In the mean time you need to move back."

"Okay. Do you know anything yet?"

"The sheriff—"

"I know. Will make a statement later." Adam returned to his SUV and threw it in reverse for about one hundred feet. He'd grown up in this town and had returned to work for the local paper after graduating college. Perhaps he should have stayed in Eugene, where life was more...interesting, but he'd chosen to come home. His parents needed his help running their lavender farm, and his high school sweetheart was here. Though she turned out to be less than sweet. She'd sure had him fooled. He'd returned home with a ring and plans to propose only to discover she'd been dating someone else.

Rachel Dillon had married the guy and then disappeared. Well not literally, but they lived outside of town and he hadn't seen her in over a year, for which he was grateful. The sky opened, and rain pounded onto his car so hard it sounded like a jackhammer inside. He turned up the wipers, doing little good to combat the incredible rain. Maybe he should return to town. The sheriff would let him know when she knew something, and it wasn't like anyone else was going to scoop him.

He signaled and after looking carefully for traffic did a U-turn then headed to Tipton. The woman's legs flashed in his mind again. If only he could un-see them. Unease clung to him like sticky tape. Did he know the victim?

Chapter Two

NANCY GLANCED TOWARD THE LIBRARY DOORS for at least the fifth time in the last fifteen minutes. Why hadn't someone come for Amelia? She glanced down at the infant sleeping soundly in her carrier. So far the little one had been quiet, but how long would it last? At least the library was slow today, probably because of the lousy weather. She couldn't sit here any longer not knowing what was going on. She'd sent Carter a text asking about the dead person since he was a deputy, but he hadn't responded.

Two women strolled into the library and dumped a stack of books into the return bin.

"Good morning."

Krista and Angie were regulars to the library and could be counted on to come in at least once a week.

"Hi." Krista unzipped her raincoat. "Can you believe this weather? I wasn't sure we were going to make it here today."

Angie chuckled. "Nothing was going to keep me away from my weekly score."

"You'd think all you do is read," Krista said.

Amelia cooed.

Krista's eyes widened. "Who's this?"

"Amelia. Her mommy left her with us."

"She's adorable and so tiny. Can I hold her? I love babies."

Angie looped her arm through her friend's. "Don't

get any ideas. I distinctly remember you telling me that Grant's not ready for kids yet."

"I only want to hold her." Krista frowned and looked longingly toward the baby.

"The next thing you know you'll be begging Grant to change his mind about having kids right now. Nope, you have a good thing going. Your time is yours. I won't let you spoil it. Let's go get some more books."

Krista sighed. "You're right." The women headed to the romance section.

The way those two went through books, Nancy would have to order several new ones soon because they were going to run out. In less than ten minutes they had each filled their canvas bags they always brought along and waited to check out.

Nancy scanned each book then sent the women on their way. In desperate need of a change in scenery, she stood, slipped into her coat, and grabbed the baby carrier holding Amelia—time to do a little investigating. She found Tara right where she'd expected. "I'm going to Roaster's Coffee. Can I get you anything?" She placed Amelia on the floor.

"A London Fog would be wonderful. I could use a treat after this morning."

"Yeah. Will you sit at the desk while I'm gone please and keep an eye on the baby? I noticed formula in Amelia's bag. She's been here for a few hours, so you might want to get a bottle ready for when she wakes up."

"How do I do that?"

"There are instructions on the can."

"It's okay to touch it now?"

"My mom already has the letter as evidence. To be honest, unless the woman's prints are in the system it won't matter. Besides, I'm sure Amelia and her mom lost priority. We can't wait forever to get her stuff from the bag."

"Oh. Okay." Tara hoisted the baby carrier and walked with Nancy back to the circulation desk.

"I won't be long." Nancy zipped up her coat and pulled the hood over her head then headed out into the stormy day. Hopefully her friend's coffee shop had power. She turned left at the end of the walkway and quickened her pace as the rain came down harder. Maybe a walk wasn't her best idea, but she needed to do something other than sit in the library and wait.

Two minutes later she entered Roaster's Coffee. The scent of freshly brewed coffee immediately relaxed her. A handful of patrons glanced her way. She smiled. "Good morning."

Pepper, the owner and Nancy's long-time friend, stood behind the counter wearing a red apron over a black sweater, talking with a woman. "Hey, there. Do you know Lacy Siletz?"

Nancy held out her hand. "Not officially. Haven't I seen you in the library?"

The tall woman grasped her hand and gave it a firm shake, impressing Nancy since she seemed on the young side—probably around twenty-one, give or take a year. "Yes, though not as often as I'd like. I'm a student so I don't have a lot of time to read for fun. I love books, but I've been buying textbooks more than anything lately. You probably recognize me from here." She pointed to a corner table. I'm parked right there on Friday mornings when you and Pepper meet for donuts.”

“Of course. I remember now. It’s nice to meet you. What school are you attending?”

“I’m mostly taking online classes except for one morning a week when I attend classes in Monmouth at Western Oregon.”

Nancy nodded. She knew the woman seemed familiar. “I’m surprised we haven’t met sooner.”

“Well, today is Monday, the day *I* often visit with Pepper. Otherwise I’m holed up behind my computer” Lacy grinned. “I’m glad you popped in. I wanted to talk with you about volunteering at the library.”

“Really?” She needed more volunteers. “That’s great. The application is on the library’s website. I’d love the help. Thanks.”

“Thank Pepper. It was her idea when I mentioned needing to find something to fill my community service hours for one of my classes.”

Nancy shot Pepper a look of appreciation. “That was so thoughtful. Thanks.”

Pepper’s cheeks pinked. “It was nothing. Don’t let her fool you with talk of textbooks. I’ve caught her reading a romance book or two. She loves to read. It was a no brainer.”

Lacy laughed “Guilty. I should go. See you later, Pepper. Thanks for the tea. I’ll be in touch, Nancy.”

Pepper waved then turned her attention to Nancy. “What brings you by on a blustery Monday?”

Nancy’s thoughts shifted back to her reason for coming. “I needed to see a friendly face as well as get a cup of your delicious coffee. Could I have a large coffee and a London fog to go?”

“Sure thing.” Pepper got busy making the drinks

but kept glancing toward Nancy. "I know you're excited about a potential new volunteer at the library but you don't seem yourself. What's going on?"

"It shows, huh? We had an unexpected guest left at the library this morning." She kept her voice low though in case her mom wanted to keep the baby off the gossip chain. "You need to keep this to yourself."

"Okay. What's going on?"

"An infant not more than a week old infant was left outside the library this morning."

"You're kidding." Pepper rested a hand on her hip.

"I wish. We're trying to figure out who her mother is. Do you recall any pregnant women coming in here in the last couple of weeks? Or even a mom and a newborn in the past few days?"

"My goodness, I don't know about pregnant women, but for sure no newborns were here. At least none that I saw. I'm more of a face person. I tend not to look below the neck."

Nancy held in a chuckle. Her petite friend had to look up at most people. One would think she'd notice a pregnant woman. But she kept busy here so maybe it made sense. "I think you'd have noticed this sweet angel."

Pepper frowned. "I wish I could help. I don't think I've ever heard of a baby being abandoned in Tipton before. What's this town coming to?"

"It's only one person, not an entire town, Pepper."

"You know what I mean." She handed her the drinks.

Nancy paid. "See you Friday. And don't forget to keep this to yourself."

"I promise."

Nancy grinned and walked out. Even though Pepper was as much a gossip as the rest of the people in this town, her word was good. If she said she wouldn't tell anyone about the baby, she wouldn't.

Stillness surrounded her. The rain and wind had finally stopped. Nancy drew in a deep breath of fresh rain-washed air as she strode toward the library. A state vehicle sat parked along the curb in front of the building. It looked like DHS had finally showed up. She was a little sad to see Amelia go, but it was for the best.

She headed inside and spotted a woman talking with Tara, who looked ready to cry—odd. Nancy had never known Tara to be weepy. Nancy sidled up to the women.

The DHS case worker reached for Amelia's diaper bag. "Is this everything?"

"I'm afraid so," Nancy said. "What's going to happen to her?"

"She'll be placed with a foster family for now. She's a pretty little thing."

Nancy nodded.

"Well, we're off." The woman, along with Amelia, left the building.

Nancy focused on Tara. "You look wiped out. Do you need to take the rest of the day off?"

"Do you mind? My car died this morning, and I need to see about getting it fixed."

"Why didn't you say something sooner?"

"My mind was otherwise occupied. Do you think Amelia will be okay?"

"I'm sure of it." She'd say about anything to clear

the worry lines off Tara's forehead.

"I hope so. Thanks for letting me go. Hopefully it's just a dead battery and an easy fix."

Nancy nodded then headed to the stacks where they'd left the book return cart earlier and finished shelving the books. By three o'clock things were hopping. Sending Tara home had been an impulse—one she regretted now, especially since her volunteers had called in sick. A line five people deep waited to check out books, not to mention the man standing at the reference counter. "I'll be with you shortly, sir."

He nodded as recognition lit his eyes. "Nancy?"

Nancy looked at him again, only this time, really looked at him. "Adam? I almost didn't recognize you behind that beard."

He chuckled. "I get that a lot. I can come back later. It looks like you're alone and might be a while."

"I am. If you don't mind waiting, I'll be done here soon." She almost sighed when someone else stepped into line.

The doors slid apart and Tara strolled inside. Her eyes widened. Cleary she didn't expect to see the place so busy. She rushed over to Nancy. "What can I do?"

Relief filled Nancy. "Will you help Adam? He's the guy standing at the reference desk.

"Sure." Tara turned and sucked in a quick breath. Where had this man been hiding? "He's cute," she whispered.

Nancy nodded. "He works for the local paper."

"A reporter?"

Nancy nodded.

"I wonder what he's doing here." Tara hesitated then scooted off to help the man. "Hi, I'm Tara, Nancy's assistant. Is there something I can help you with?"

The reporter nodded. "Yes. Thank you." He held out his hand. "I'm Adam, a reporter for the Tipton Tribune. I'm doing a story on the history of crime in Tipton County. It will be a then and now kind of thing. Unfortunately, the Tribune's archives weren't much help thanks to a fire in the early 80s."

"That's an interesting topic. What inspired you?"

"The hit and run victim."

His tone gave her pause and she noted the furrow of his brow. His full beard hid his mouth, but his soulful brown eyes spoke volumes. "Did you know her?"

He cleared his throat and shrugged. "Since I grew up here I'm guessing I might have, but the identity of the victim has not yet been released."

It must be horrible not knowing. Hopefully it wasn't anyone he knew. Death was always a tragedy, but when you knew the person it was so much worse. "It's been quite a day in Tipton. I found an abandoned baby on my way into the library this morning."

"You're kidding?"

Maybe she shouldn't have said anything about Amelia. Oh well, too late now. "I wouldn't kid about something like that." Her breath hitched when his gaze slammed into hers. Why did he have to be so good looking and smell so shower fresh? She tore her gaze from his and turned to the blank computer screen. "Is the computer not working?"

He jiggled the mouse. "Must have fallen asleep. Does the library keep records of the crimes in Tipton County?"

"I'm not sure. No one has ever asked." She glanced toward Nancy and breathed easier. The last person in line walked away. She motioned for her boss to join them.

"What are you researching?" Nancy asked.

"Crime statistics, but it appears no one has kept online records for Tipton. Perhaps there's something on microfiche." Tara's heart went out to the man beside her. She suspected he was dealing with his grief about the hit and run by doing what he probably knew best—writing about it.

"There's a box in the storage room." Nancy winced. "My mom asked me to transfer the records to the computer quite a while back, but I never finished. I'm afraid solving current-day mysteries along with running this place has kept me busy."

"Tara told me about the abandoned baby. I don't think I've heard of that happening here before."

"To my knowledge it hasn't. But my mom doesn't tell me everything. I doubt I'd have known about Amelia if it hadn't been for the fact she was left on our doorstep. Out of respect for the baby, I hope you will keep that out of the paper and on the down low. We aren't making it public."

Tara's stomach knotted. "I'm sorry. I didn't realize that."

"It's okay, but for now, we need to keep it quiet."

"Understood." He rubbed his beard. "Doesn't that make you curious though?" Adam asked. "Why here? Of all the places a baby could be left the mother chose the library. What's the connection? Is there a connection?"

Nancy grimaced. "You ask a lot of questions."

"Occupational hazard."

Tara had been asking the same things. Why had Amelia been left here and not the diner, or a church or any number of other places?

"I imagine you're wired to dig deeper," Nancy said. "I'm much the same. I have a hard time leaving well enough alone."

"Uh-oh," Tara said. "I see that look on your face. You're not going to let the authorities handle this are you?"

"Of course I will. But I'll do a little sleuthing on my own."

Adam chuckled. "You haven't changed a bit since we were kids."

Nancy stuck out her tongue, causing him to laugh harder. "Case closed."

He looked at Tara. "Thanks for your help. I should go write my article—I have a plan B. I haven't missed a deadline, and I don't plan to start today."

Tara nodded. "Good luck." Her gaze followed him all the way to the door.

Nancy twittered. "You like him."

"What's not to like? He's cute, smart, and he's really nice." But so was Patrick and he proved to be the biggest mistake of her life. She tucked her hands into her pockets. "I can stay for the rest of the day, in case it gets crazy here again."

"Is your car fixed?"

She nodded. "Turned out to be the battery."

"You didn't try to jump it?"

"I don't own jumper cables." And she'd never gotten to know her neighbors, so she hadn't sought out help.

"Girl, that's standard equipment." Nancy shook her head. "I think I have a spare in my garage. It's all yours."

"Thanks, but I have a new battery now. It better not die."

"You never know."

"I suppose." Tara looked toward the door again and bit down on her bottom lip. In the short amount of time she'd spent with Adam she got a good vibe from him and actually liked him, which was shocking considering his profession. Then again, her instincts couldn't be trusted. She'd learned that the hard way and had paid the price ever since.

Nancy sat in her mom's office in the basement of the courthouse. Carter and Lyle each flanked the doorway. "I don't understand why I can't know the identity of the person you found."

"We have to notify next of kin," her mom said.

"But you always tell me about your cases."

"Things are different this time."

"Why?"

"This isn't a case of stolen license plates, Nancy." Carter crossed his arms.

"Duh. But I don't see how that matters." She made a silly face. He was supposed to be on her side, but it seemed whenever it came to a police matter, he chose to side with her mom. Then again, her mom was his boss, so she couldn't really hold it against him.

"Now, Nancy." Lyle shook his head. "You're given a lot of leeway here, but you have to admit most of the things that come through this department aren't life and death. This case is different, and you need to stay out of it."

Nancy crossed her arms. "Fine." If they were going to gang up on her she'd move on. "What about the investigation into Amelia's mom. I could help with that."

"Actually," her mom said, "that's a good idea. We have our hands full with this other case. I'll forward you anything we learn."

Nancy grinned. "I appreciate your faith in me. I think this is the most serious case you've ever sent my way."

"I'm sure of it. But don't get too excited. You're still indefinitely off any case that involves danger."

Nancy shrugged. She wasn't a thrill seeker unless you counted the thrill of finding and following leads, or driving too fast. "Understood." Her stomach growled. "That reminds me. I put a roast in the crockpot this morning. There's plenty for all of you—assuming the power didn't go out and mess it up."

"I'd love to Nancy," Carter rubbed the back of his neck. "But I'm working late tonight."

She shifted in her seat to better see him. "You're working the homicide."

"No one said it was murder." Lyle wagged a finger at her. "Anyone ever tell you you're relentless?"

"Maybe." She grinned. "There are worse things to be. Isn't hit and run pretty much murder if the person dies?"

"You know better than to ask that, Nancy," Lyle stuffed a hand into his pocket.

"Fine. If you're going to be picky." She shot him a cheeky grin and stood. "The offer stands if any of you can make it." She used to enjoy her time alone, but she had grown accustomed to having someone around when her neighbor Anna had lived at her place this past spring. She squeezed Carter's hand as she passed him. A look of longing that she was certain matched her own filled his eyes. She missed him even though they'd spent most of Sunday together.

Once they were married she imagined that would change, as they'd be living under the same roof. Of course it would be quite an adjustment having a teenager underfoot, since his nephew Gavin was part of the deal. He was a good kid for the most part and a junior in high school, so it wouldn't be long and he'd be off to college.

Nancy got into her classic Mustang, which she had parked on the end so only one car would have the chance to bang its door into her new-to-her ride. She still couldn't believe Carter had found the same model and year to replace hers after a racing teenager who'd run a red light had totaled her car. She missed that car, but the fact that Carter went to so much trouble to locate a car just like her old one, was so heartwarming that she would treasure it for as long as she could.

She headed home, being extra careful at intersections. She did not want a repeat incident, even if it meant she had to ease off the gas a bit to allow for more response time.

She slowed as she came up to her house then pulled into the driveway. Anna, her dear friend and next-door neighbor, headed in her direction, wearing her walking clothes. They'd been walking buddies for the past year and tonight would be no exception. Nancy got out. "Sorry I'm late. I'll go change. Come on in." She hustled toward the front door not waiting to see if Anna followed then raced inside, leaving the door wide open. Anna would close it.

After changing and making sure her dinner was still cooking in the crockpot, Nancy locked up and they headed out. She pumped her arms as she walked at a brisk pace. Since it was fall, by the time they returned it would be dark, but the streetlamps would light their way. Her thoughts drifted over her conversation with her mother. She had never tried to find a mom who didn't want to be found. This was vastly different than anything she'd ever had to figure out. Where should she begin?

"Was the library busy today?" Anna asked.

"Only after the storm passed. Did the school lose power?"

"For a little while, but thankfully not long enough that we had to send everyone home. I hate losing a day of teaching."

"Spoken like a true educator." What if the baby's mom had been a teenager? "I want to tell you something but it's between you and me okay? I'd like to keep this off the town gossip train."

"Sure." Anna looked her way, her brow furrowed. "What's going on?"

"A baby was abandoned outside the library today."

Anna gasped. "That's horrible."

"I agree. I'm trying to track down the mom, and it occurred to me this might be something a teenager would do."

"I agree, but an adult is just as likely. I don't remember seeing any pregnant girls at school this year, but that doesn't mean there weren't any."

"How about a girl that's been wearing baggy or lose fitting clothes."

Anna shot her look. "Lots of girls dress like that."

"Okay. What about one that didn't use to dress like that but does now?"

"I don't know. I'll have to think on it for a while. I wouldn't know about the freshman."

"Right."

"I'm surprised you didn't catch the woman on video surveillance, considering how you have cameras all over." Anna pumped her arms harder and increased her pace.

Nancy matched her speed. "The power was out for about thirty minutes. She must have come then. Amelia was found behind a planter. At least she was in a covered area."

Anna shook her head. "It boggles the mind that someone would leave a precious baby outside in that kind of weather. I think we need to educate girls about the law regarding abandoning their newborn."

"I agree. I might bring that up to Titus the next time I see him." The new principal at Tipton High School was a friend of her fiancés, and hers by default.

"Or I can."

"You don't mind?" Anna and Titus had dated

briefly last school year.

"Not at all. In fact, I'll bring it up at the next staff meeting. That baby's mother might very well not be a teenager, but it's still good to make sure our students are educated." Anna waved at a passing car.

"A friend?" Nancy asked.

"A former student. Have you checked with the businesses near the library? Just because the library lost power doesn't mean the businesses on the other side of the street did."

"I like how you think. I could use a partner to bounce theories off of."

"Count me in."

Nancy knew Anna would jump at the suggestion. She should include Tara too. The woman had seemed especially fond of little Amelia. "When are you free? I thought my library assistant might want to help too."

"I could be there at four tomorrow."

"I'm usually busy then, but that will give you time to visit with Tara and toss ideas around." Meanwhile she'd make a few calls tonight to see about those security cameras. Perhaps she'd get lucky and the woman would be revealed.

Chapter Three

THE FOLLOWING EVENING, NANCY SNUGGLED INTO Carter's side as they sat on her sofa. "I don't see any good reason why you can't tell me the identity of the dead woman."

"Of course you don't." He chuckled. "Like your mom said, once the next of kin has been notified, her identity will be made public."

"Sweet junipers. What harm is there in telling me. It's not like I'm going to alert the press."

He shifted, causing Nancy to sit up. "I'd much rather talk about us. As in when you and I are going to get married."

All sensical thought fled Nancy's mind. He'd proposed in the spring and here it was October and they'd yet to set a date.

"Don't you want to marry me?" Hurt filled his voice.

"Of course I do. But I like being engaged. It's fun telling everyone you're my fiancé." She really wanted to marry him, but for whatever reason she resisted setting a date. A wedding was a huge ordeal that she simply didn't have the time, patience, or desire to deal with.

"I like being engaged to you too, but I'd enjoy being married to you more." The longing in his eyes spoke his thoughts.

"We could elope."

"I want a real wedding with all the trimmings."

"Trimmings, huh?" Nancy's throat went dry. She licked her lips. "How about a Christmas wedding? You said you want the trimmings."

His brow rose. "Are you serious? You realize that's less than two months away?"

She nodded. How would she plan a wedding and find Amelia's mom, as well as do her job at the library?

"Then Christmas it is." He pulled her close and claimed her lips for a toe tingling moment. "Gavin will be excited. He's looking forward to eating someone else's cooking."

Nancy rolled her eyes. "Is that all I'm good for? A meal? I'm not even a great cook."

"I disagree." His lips found her again.

She could get accustomed to this. Somehow she'd figure out how to do everything.

Two days after the woman was found, Adam stood outside the courthouse listening to the sheriff's press release, with his phone set to record.

"On Monday the body of Rachel Dillon was found deceased due to vehicular homicide on the side of highway 99. That's all we have."

Adam sucked in a sharp breath. Rachel? His Rachel was dead? Well, she wasn't his, but still... "Excuse me, Sheriff Daley. What is being done to find the person who hit her?"

"No comment." Her face softened. "You knew the victim didn't you?"

"How'd you know?"

"I have been in this town a long time. I make it my business to know things."

"But we were only kids in high school."

She shrugged. "My daughter is close to your age."

He nodded. "If there's anything I can do to help, please let me know." Rachel might have broken his heart, but no one deserved to die like that. Her killer needed to be held accountable.

"I will." She studied him a moment. "You okay?"

"I'm shocked but otherwise fine. I haven't seen Rachel for a few years. Do you think she was hit intentionally?"

The sheriff paused, then without answering walked inside the courthouse building.

Well, she had said no comment, so he shouldn't feel slighted. He turned and trudged back toward the Tipton Tribune office. This might be one of the most difficult stories he'd ever had to write.

The woman from the library walked toward him with a bounce in her step. Her chin length honey colored hair swung with each step. She smiled as she approached him. Her ice blue eyes met his as she pulled ear buds from her ears. "Hi, there. How's the research coming?"

Tara had an ordinary look about her—nothing really stood out, almost as if she tried to blend in and go unnoticed, but when one looked closely, she was quite beautiful. "My research is stalled at the moment. The sheriff just announced the identity of the woman found dead on the side of the road."

The happiness she'd oozed only a second ago faded. "And?"

He rubbed the back of his neck. *And she was the love of my life at one time.* He thought he was past the hurt of her rejection. Of course, he'd be sad at her life ending so suddenly, but why did her death sting to such a degree?

"Are you okay?" Tara's forehead puckered.

"Not really. The woman killed was an old friend. An old girlfriend, actually. I hadn't seen her in quite some time. It's a shock."

She touched his arm for a moment then pulled away as if shocked with her action. "I understand. Losing someone you once cared about is difficult."

Her tone suggested she'd been through it. The reporter in him wanted to dig deeper. "Are you on a break?"

She nodded. "I like to circle the block to get in some exercise when I can get away."

"So coffee is out?"

She shook her head. "I don't drink coffee, but I could be persuaded to stop for tea."

She reversed course and they ambled to Roaster's Coffee. "Tell me about your friend."

"There's not much to tell. We dated in high school. After graduating college I came home to propose, and she was with another guy."

She winced. "Ouch. You must have a big heart if her death upsets you."

He shot her a sideways glance. "I've discovered that holding a grudge hurts me a lot more than the person who wronged me."

"Good point, but it's hard to let go of hurts."

He tipped his head to the side. "I didn't say it was easy. Once upon a time I loved her and wanted the best for her. I thought that was me, but she didn't agree, so I walked away."

"Wow. Not sure I would have been so gracious." She paused outside the coffee shop.

He pulled open the door. "After you."

"Thanks."

Thankfully there wasn't a line at the counter. He didn't imagine Tara had too long of a break. "What would you like? My treat."

"That's nice. Thanks. I'd like a mint tea, please. I'll get yours next time." She stuffed the ten-dollar bill she had pulled out back into her pocket.

He ordered a coffee with room for cream then paid. "Do you have time to sit, or do you need to keep walking?"

She checked her watch. "I need to keep moving. Sorry."

"No problem. I'll walk with you. I could use some fresh air." He was stalling, pure and simple. But the walk would give him time to chew on the news the sheriff had delivered and figure out how to spin his article. He quickly added cream and sugar to his coffee then popped on a lid and headed for the door alongside Tara. "How did you come to work at the library?"

"Same as anyone else. I applied and got the job."

He chuckled at the flippant reply. "And to think I went to college and earned a degree in journalism when all I really needed to do was apply."

She grinned. "Sorry. I suppose you meant why I chose that field?"

"That'd be a good start."

"I love books."

"It's really that simple?" He didn't buy it. She'd come across as open before, but the moment he wanted more details she withdrew. What was up with that? Trust issues perhaps?

"For me it is. Since I was a girl the feel and smell of the pages made me happy. Working in a library made sense."

"What about a book store?"

"The library was hiring when I needed a job. Speaking of which." She had stopped on the sidewalk in front of the library. "We should do this again."

His brain stalled. "Uh...yeah. Sure. Sounds good. I'd like that."

She rested a hand on his arm again, this time not seeming to be in any hurry to remove it. "I'm sorry about your friend. If you need someone to talk to, I'm a good listener."

He stood a little taller. "Thanks. I appreciate the offer. I might take you up on it sometime. Enjoy the books." He pivoted and headed to his office. His boss would be wondering what happened to him. He pulled out his phone and sent off a voice text then pocketed his phone and sipped his coffee.

He couldn't get Tara off his mind even though he needed to formulate a rough outline for his article. The woman intrigued him. There was definitely more to her than met the eye.

Tara breezed into the library after her walk with Adam and found Nancy in her usual spot behind the checkout counter visiting with a woman. Her boss truly enjoyed visiting with the library patrons. Not that Tara was anti-social, but she never could muster up the desire for small talk with each and every person she came into contact with, the way Nancy did. The woman had a gift for getting people to open up. Good thing she'd never gotten past Tara's walls or she'd have to start fresh someplace else, and she rather liked Tipton—especially the local newspaper reporter.

She'd have to watch herself with him though. The fact that she liked him and wanted to spend time with him shot off alarms—her track record stunk and she couldn't afford to mess up again.

Nancy looked her direction when she sat beside her. "Did you have a nice walk?" she kept her voice low even though the woman she'd been talking with had wandered off.

"I did." Tara still needed to drink her tea. Technically food and drink were a no-no in the library, but Nancy allowed beverages with a cover and the occasional sandwich. She sipped the tea, which had thankfully cooled. "I ran into that reporter who was in here on Monday. He knew the woman who was left for dead on the side of the road."

"How sad." Nancy processed returned books into the computer. "Did they say the cause of death?"

"I assumed it was a hit and run."

"You never know."

"I suppose." Tara stood. "I should get back to work." She motioned toward a cart filled with books. "Are those ready for me to reshelf."

Nancy nodded. "When you're finished with that, there are some books that need to be mended."

"Okay." Tara reached for the next book to shelf. The picture of a baby stared back at her. Her thoughts flew to Amelia. What would come of that sweet little baby? If only she could help. But the personal cost would be too great.

Chapter Four

NANCY PUMPED HER ARMS BESIDE ANNA as they power-walked through their neighborhood. A light sprinkle fell from the clouds, but not enough to soak them. "Why the library?"

"Excuse me?" Anna looked her direction.

"The baby. Why was she left at the library? Do I know the mom and that's why she chose there to leave her?"

"It's possible. You know a great deal of the townspeople. But keep in mind, it could as easily be an out-of-towner passing through."

Nancy shook her head. "I don't think so. Amelia was cared for. She was clean and her mom made sure she left a supply of items to care for her. I don't think someone who loved her baby enough to do that would leave her under the awning of a random library. No, this person knew her baby would be taken care of and more importantly that the library would be open."

"You make a good point. But how does it help? You know a ton of people."

"Honestly, I don't know, but it makes me feel like I'm making progress." All of the businesses around the library had lost power at the same time she had, so no one had footage of the time in question. The one bright spot was they were willing to let her view the video surveillance leading up to the power outage.

Her feed hadn't shown anyone, but maybe the woman had hovered nearby but out of range to be seen, contemplating what she was about to do. Nancy sure hoped so.

"Speaking of feeling better, I'm sorry for being a no-show at the library the other day. Something came up at work, and I couldn't get away."

"Is everything okay? No more problems I hope." Anna had been through the wringer last spring after being falsely accused of helping students cheat. Thankfully, her name had been cleared, but a few parents still caused her problems. Apparently, accused meant guilty, period, to some people, even if said person was exonerated and the guilty party confessed.

"Nothing serious. But I had to deal with something that took longer than I expected."

Hmm. Anna was usually more forthcoming. What was she hiding? Nancy shook her head at her suspicious mind. Anna would tell her if she needed to know.

"I think you might be onto something about knowing the baby's mom. You didn't notice any pregnant women in the library in the past couple of months?"

"I'm sure there were, but no one stands out in my mind." She took pride in being observant, but it appeared she wasn't as observant as she'd once thought. "Oh, and on top of this case, I also need to plan our wedding."

"You finally set a date?"

"Not a date, but we did decide on a Christmas wedding."

"So when would that make it? Christmas Eve?" Anna asked.

"What a great idea. We could hold it after the Christmas service at church. I'll have to talk with our pastor and see if that will work. Thanks for the idea." Doing it after the service would sure save prep time and money. They'd use the church's *trimmings*. She chuckled. Carter had no idea what he'd started by using that word.

"Are you sure you don't want to make it your own? I know a good wedding coordinator."

"Thanks. I'm going to keep things simple. I doubt there'd be enough work to hire a coordinator."

Anna looked at her like she'd grown a second head.

"What?" The church would already be decorated; she'd get Pepper to make the cake and their pastor to marry them. What more was there? She could still make the wedding her own even if they did use the church's Christmas decorations.

"Nancy?"

"Hmm."

"Have you heard anything I've said in the last minute?"

"I guess not."

Anna laughed. "You must be scheming then. I've noticed how you tune everyone out when you're plotting something."

"I don't plot." Nancy laughed at the ridiculous direction their conversation had taken.

"Ha! And I don't teach sophomore English."

Nancy rolled her eyes. "Whatever."

"Now you look and sound like one of my students.

Speaking of which, I was able to talk with Titus, and he supports the idea of adding the Safe Haven law to the curriculum."

"Wonderful. That's really great news. It's nice to see something good come of a bad situation." Titus was proving to be an excellent principal at the high school. But great news didn't solve the case. She needed to figure this out and fast so she could focus on her wedding. Maybe she wasn't one of those women who had dreamed of her wedding her entire life, but she loved Carter, and this was important to him, so it was important to her. One way or another, she'd make sure they had the wedding he wanted.

Tara sat across from Adam at Roaster's Coffee. She sipped mint tea while he held a steaming cup of coffee between his hands. "This is nice."

"As nice as a jaunt around the block?" Adam raised the cup to his lips.

He'd trimmed his beard since she'd last seen him. He looked even more handsome than before. Funny, since she'd never been a fan of facial hair.

"It's a nice change," Tara said. "Although I might regret skipping my walk." She faced the door and noticed a man she didn't recognize walk in. Her heart rate kicked up a notch. "Do you know that man who just walked in?"

Adam shifted and casually looked toward the door. "Maybe. He looks familiar, but I can't put a name with the face. Why?"

She shrugged. "No particular reason. It's unusual

to see strangers in here." Plus he gave her a look that sent chills skittering down her back.

He shook his head. "You were a stranger here once, yet look at you now."

His smile warmed her. She dipped her chin and focused on Adam—at least he didn't give her the creeps like that other man. Aside from being a reporter, Adam seemed perfect. Was she playing with fire by getting to know him? She'd grown accustomed to the loneliness of her new life in Tipton—even liked it. She loved her life here and didn't want to do anything to mess it up. Would Adam prove to be her kryptonite? She desperately hoped not because she enjoyed his company.

"Did you read the paper today?"

"Not yet. Does it include your article on crime in Tipton?"

"I ended up blending two article ideas into one since I couldn't find the historical statistics I needed. It's a piece about Rachel, her life growing up here from a former boyfriend's perspective. I included the current crime stats I had in the piece."

"Interesting."

"Interesting good or bad?"

She shrugged. "Neither. I'm surprised you didn't seek out her family and interview them."

He frowned. "I probably should have, but I couldn't get myself to intrude on their grief. I know how hard her death hit me, and I haven't seen or spoken to her since I first moved back to town." He shrugged. "I didn't want to sensationalize their grief or cause them to feel worse by asking for an interview they might not have been up to giving."

"I think I like you even more for that. You're a kind man, Adam." She stood. "Walk with me back to the library?" Surely there was no harm in spending a little extra time with Adam. Besides, the strange man she'd pointed out earlier gave her the creeps, and she didn't want to be alone.

"Sure." He grabbed his coffee, and they left together.

The man's gaze followed them as they passed by his seat at the window. His eyes narrowed, drawing attention to a scar above his right cheekbone. She shivered. Too bad Adam couldn't place him. But if he was from around here, she shouldn't need to stress about him.

"The police don't seem to have a clue who struck and killed Rachel," Adam said.

"I'm sure they'll figure it out."

"I'm not so confident. I don't recall anything like this happening in Tipton or the surrounding area. How would they even know where to start?"

She glanced his way. "You're serious. Don't you watch crime TV? They'll follow the clues."

"But what if there are no clues?"

"There are always clues. My boss happens to be an amateur sleuth, and if I've learned anything from watching her solve puzzles, it's that there is always at least one clue. I imagine the police are being tight lipped, so they don't tip their hand." If anyone knew anything it would be Nancy. She'd be sure to quiz her before heading home today.

"I like your optimism." He stopped at the same spot he'd walked her to last time. "Would you care to get dinner with me sometime?"

Her heartbeat skipped. "Like on a date?"

He nodded.

She grinned. "I'd enjoy that." When he didn't suggest a day and time disappointment filled her, but she refused to let him know. She pulled out her phone and opened it to her contacts. "I'll add my number to your phone, and you can add yours to mine." What was she doing? What if she'd misjudged him? What if he turned out to be trouble? But it was only dinner, and she was lonely. What harm could come from that?

"Great idea." He typed his number into her phone while she did the same on his.

"See you." She tucked her phone away then darted inside. The library hummed with activity, but nothing that Nancy couldn't handle so Tara got busy in the stacks shelving books. It seemed to be an endless task. She waved to Nancy as she moved past her desk. All things considered, she felt very fortunate to be working with the woman. She was kind-hearted but tough, and most importantly, Nancy made her feel safe. A feeling she missed when she wasn't in the confines of these walls.

"Tara?" Nancy walked toward her.

She turned and smiled. "What's up?"

"My friend Anna and I are getting together later to come up with a plan to find Amelia's mom. Do you still want to help us?"

Her heart skipped a beat. Nancy never involved her in one of her *cases.* "Of course. So there hasn't been any progress on locating her mom?"

"I'm afraid not. Our local law enforcement is stretched thin right now with the hit and run."

"It was confirmed a hit and run, not a body dump?"

"That's my understanding. What made you think otherwise?"

Tara shrugged. "No reason." Great, now Nancy looked at her with suspicion-clouded eyes. "I like watching crime shows on TV. I guess my imagination works overtime." With good reason!

Nancy's eyes cleared. "We'll make quite a team then. I'm headed out for lunch. Will you take over for me?"

"Sure thing." She plastered on a smile. The only time she didn't like her job was when Nancy took a break. She felt vulnerable all alone, but Nancy said the budget didn't allow for any more paid staff.

Nancy left as the man from the coffee shop walked in. Tara sucked in a sharp breath.

Adam pressed send and shot off his latest article to his editor. His visit with Tara had energized his inner muse, and he'd whipped out the piece in record time. Now what? He'd accomplished all his tasks for the day. He might as well knock off early.

A short time later he strolled into the library. It had been a long time since he'd enjoyed a good book—according to his sources this library had a nice selection of mysteries. He could use the distraction.

Silence filled the space—not so unusual for a library, but something felt off. It was too quiet. Where was everyone? He moved toward the stacks and looked down each row. A man wearing a long brown trench coat crept around the corner of one. Adam's pulse amped—something was definitely not right.

On impulse he started to whistle, "Amazing Grace." Maybe if the man knew someone was approaching he wouldn't do anything rash. Something crashed to the floor. He darted forward and looked down the row where the man had disappeared. Several large books lay on the floor, but there was no sign of him—had he made a run for it? He whistled softer, staining to hear footsteps—nothing.

Where was Tara? He'd spotted Nancy on his way here, so Tara must be in the building somewhere. He turned and jolted when someone smacked into him. He thrust out his hands and captured the shoulders of..."Tara? You're shaking. Are you okay?" He kept his voice low, not wishing to be overheard by the creepy man should he be nearby.

"I am now that you're here."

He strained to hear her quiet voice. "What's going on?"

"That man from the coffee shop is here, and he scares me."

He grasped Tara's hand. "I don't think you're in any danger. Let's go sit a the circulation desk."

She yanked her hand free. "No. We'll be sitting ducks."

He winced inwardly at her much-used cliché. As a writer it had been engrained in his mind to avoid clichés, but he shouldn't hold a non-writer to the same standard. "Did he threaten you?"

"No, but something feels off with him."

"I agree. Call Nancy but let's not overreact." Every

instinct in him said the man was up to no good. And like it or not, Tara was right—they were sitting ducks if the dude was armed and he intended to harm Tara. But why would he want to harm her? It didn't make sense.

"Can we please go outside instead of the circulation desk until Nancy returns?" Her eyes pleaded with him. "There's no one here but us and that man, and I'm scared."

"I suppose it wouldn't hurt. Let's go." He held out his hand, waiting for her to take it. Her cold fingers wrapped around his hand. They strolled to the circulation desk. He stopped and looked around. No sign of the man—had he sneaked out a back door after dropping the books? Had the books crashing to the floor been a distraction, giving the man time to slip out? "I don't see him, do you?" he asked out of the side of his mouth.

"No."

"Do you have your phone?"

She nodded.

He pivoted and headed toward the exit, never loosening his grip on Tara. He had no idea what was going on, but he certainly wasn't going to leave her alone. At least from outside they'd be able to see when the guy left, assuming he was still there. He strode to a nearby bench and sat. Good—the bench was dry.

Tara pulled out her phone and spoke to it. "Call Nancy." She was quiet for a moment. "Nancy, can you come back to the library?"

He didn't have to strain to hear the other end of the conversation since her volume was turned up.

"What's going on?"

"There's a man inside that makes me feel very uncomfortable."

"Does that mean you're no longer in the library?"

"Yes. I'm sorry. Adam is here and he thought we should leave."

"I'm on my way. Are you sure he's still inside?"

"As sure as I can be without having eyes on the emergency exit."

"Okay. I'll call Carter and be there soon."

She held her phone between her hands which rested in her lap. At some point she'd slipped free from his grasp, but he'd been listening so intently he hadn't noticed. "Where's the emergency exit?"

"On the side of the building. We can't see it from here. Nancy's calling Carter. At least we'll have the man on video since Nancy is a surveillance freak. Who do you think he is?"

"I wish I knew." He was good with faces, and though he seemed familiar, this man's identity eluded him. Whoever he was, he seemed to have an unhealthy interest in Tara. He'd noticed the man's attentiveness at the coffee shop and shrugged it off to a man admiring a pretty lady, but this was something altogether different.

Chapter Five

NANCY SAT INSIDE THE LIBRARY WITH Tara to her right and Adam to her left. Carter stood behind her, looking at the computer screen over her shoulder. The man, whoever he was, had disappeared. One minute he was on the screen, and the next, he ducked out of view and had managed to avoid the other surveillance cameras. "He must have left through the side emergency exit."

"Did he threaten you in anyway, Tara?" Carter asked.

"No, but I felt threatened. Or maybe intimidated would be a better word. We first saw him at the coffee shop. He stared at me through the window when we were walking away. He has a scar right here." She ran a finger up from her cheekbone to below her eye. "Then he showed up here. I've never seen him before, but Adam recognized him."

Adam shook his head. "Not really. He only seemed familiar. I have no idea who he is, and he made me uneasy too when I saw him skulking around the stacks."

"Did you notice a weapon on him?" Carter pulled out a notepad and pencil.

"No." Adam leaned forward and looked at Tara. "How about you?"

"No. Who do you think he is?"

"Not a clue," Carter said, "but I'll have Nancy

send this file to our IT specialist to run through facial recognition."

"It's about time the department joined this century and acquired an IT guru." Nancy clicked the computer keys. "Sent."

"Thanks." Carter gave a brief nod. "Are either of you missing anything? I know you keep your purses under the desk."

"I haven't noticed anything missing," Tara looked around the space.

"Me either." Nancy shook her head.

"Good. Until we find this guy, pay attention to your surroundings and don't go out alone. The adage that there's safety in numbers still rings true." Carter pocketed his notepad.

"But I live alone." Fear filled Tara's voice.

Nancy rubbed her back. "We'll figure it out. A security system would give you peace of mind while you're home. Or if it would make you feel better you can crash at my place."

"That's really nice of you to offer, but I don't want to put you out. My biggest concern is running errands and going to and from work."

"I don't mind giving you a lift," Adam said. "And I'm more than happy to accompany you on your breaks."

Nancy's head shifted from side to side. She really needed to get out of the middle and let them talk. Tara's refusal to stay with her was no surprise—they weren't close.

Carter tapped her shoulder. "I need to head out."

"Okay." Nancy rolled her chair back and stood. "I'll walk you out." She had a theory she wanted to run past him. A strong breeze whipped her hair into her face as they left the library. "Do you think the man who came here has anything to do with baby Amelia? What if he's the dad?"

"Then why follow Tara? Clearly she doesn't have her."

"No, but she's the one who found her and brought her inside. What if he was watching? And now he's trying to get close to Tara to learn about his daughter."

"Why leave the baby here if he cared that much? Plus, the chances that a man dropped off that infant is minimal."

"I don't know. Maybe he had a change of heart. The more I think about it, the more I like him for it."

Carter chuckled and pulled her into his arms.

She relaxed into him. "This is nice."

He kissed the top of her head. "I agree, but—"

"You have to go. I know." She tilted her head back and kissed him quickly. "We need to work on our wedding plans. Want to come over for dinner tonight and figure some things out?"

He replied with a lopsided grin. "See you later."

Nancy chuckled and headed inside. For law enforcement, her fiancé was mighty easy to read. Carter was right about the man being a long shot as the dad, but what if he was? She needed to find him to know for sure. She knew most of the people in this town and didn't recognize him at all. Why had Adam thought he was familiar? Time to find out.

Adam and Tara still sat where she'd left them. She walked over and sat on the corner of her desk. "I'm curious what it was about the man that seemed familiar to you, Adam?"

"I wish I knew. It was a general feeling, but now I'm not so sure."

"Perhaps you ran into him while doing something work related."

"Maybe." He rubbed his chin. His face brightened. "Actually, I think that's it. I'm also the paper's photographer so maybe I took his picture for an article at one time, or he was in the background. I don't usually forget a face." He stood. "I'm going to follow up on this now. I'll swing by later and follow you home, Tara."

"Okay, thanks."

Nancy waited until he'd left the building then crossed her arms and looked at Tara. "Is there something going on between the two of you?"

"Not yet."

"So you like him."

"What's not to like? He's practically perfect."

Nancy chuckled as she stood. "Only practically?" He did have a certain je ne sais quoi about him, not that she was even remotely interested in the man, but she could understand why her assistant was attracted to him.

"Well, he *is* a reporter."

Nancy snort-laughed. "What do you have against reporters?"

"They're excellent researchers." Tara stood. "I'll be in the stacks."

Nancy watched her hasty retreat, pondering Tara's statement. Why would she be bothered by his researching skills unless she was afraid he'd discover something she didn't want him to know? Did Tara have cobwebs in her past? Carter had been suspicious of her when he'd first come to town, but Nancy had defended her, and she would do the same now. Tara was not a criminal; she knew it in her bones. It appeared her employee was afraid of something being discovered, but what?

Adam parked beside Tara's car in the driveway of a duplex. She got out, and he joined her beside the hood of her car. "I'll wait until you get inside and give me the all clear before I leave."

Relief covered her face. "Thanks. I'm sorry for causing you so much trouble. Before I go in, did you figure out why that guy looked familiar to you?"

"No, and I looked through all the photos I've taken over the past month." Maybe the man had one of those familiar kind of faces, because he'd scoured through the pictures until his eyes turned bleary.

"I don't mind. The only thing I have planned for this evening is thawing a frozen meal for dinner and research for a story idea." He enjoyed cooking, and once a month he prepared several dinners to keep in the freezer for nights like this when he didn't have the time to cook something fresh.

"What kind of story?"

He shook his head. "I don't like to talk about what I'm mulling over."

"Okay." She turned and headed for the entrance on the right then disappeared inside. She poked her head back out. "Everything looks fine here. Thanks again for following me home."

He waved then hopped into his SUV and left. He hadn't been completely honest with Tara. Yes, he had research to do this evening, but it wasn't work related. He wanted to know Tara's story. Where she came from and how she came to live in Tipton. He'd tried to get the information from her, but every time he'd broached the questions, she'd changed to another topic. There had to be a reason, and he aimed to find out.

He drove straight home, went directly to his home office then powered on his computer. It would take a few minutes for the dinosaur to come to life, so he headed for the kitchen to thaw and heat his dinner in the microwave.

He pulled open the freezer door and reached for the top container. He had a system. He had stacked his dinners in random order and pulled from the top. This way it was always a surprise, and he never had the same meal twice in a row should he have an extra busy week with no time or energy to cook a fresh meal. Tonight was enchiladas—his favorite.

Two hours later, he propped his elbows on his desk and rested his head in his hands. How was it possible that he couldn't find any trace of Tara online before she came to Tipton? The only person he could find with her name didn't look anything like her. It was as though she didn't exist. Had she stolen someone's identity? No. If that were the case, he would have discovered it already. He had a friend at the FBI who might be able to help, except this wasn't research for a story—it was personal. He liked Tara, but something wasn't right. She had no backstory online. Everyone had some kind of history. So why couldn't he find anything on her? He couldn't even find her on social media—at least no one who resembled her going by Tara James. Maybe she'd had cosmetic surgery and that's why she didn't look like the woman online that he would have expected to be her.

He liked a mystery as much as the next person, but he'd wasted enough time. He reached for his phone and dialed. "Jason, long time no speak."

"Who's this?"

Uh-oh, he should have kept in better touch with his old college roommate. "Adam. Has my voice changed?"

"Sorry. A head cold is plaguing me, and my ears are plugged. How's it going? You still in your hometown?"

"I am. How about you?" Adam asked.

"Seattle."

"Cool. You were hoping for a spot there. Congrats."

"Thanks. Plugged ears or not I can tell this isn't a casual call."

"You always could read me. I need help getting background on a woman."

Jason chuckled. "This is a first. Someone has finally caught your attention?"

"Maybe. She's cagey about her past, and the reporter in me can't let it go. Then there's this dude who came into her place of employment. He gave us both the creeps. I saw him skulking around the stacks at the library where she works, and my gut says he was up to no good. Can you help?"

"I could get in trouble."

"I wouldn't ask if it wasn't important." Something wasn't right with Tara, and he couldn't rest until he figured out what. Plus, that man wasn't in the library for a book. He was up to something—what and why?

"Fine, but you owe me big time. Give me her name and address. If you have her date of birth even better."

"Anything you need, ask. And thanks." Adam rattled off her name and current address. "I don't know her birthdate."

"Okay. I'll see what I can find. Hang tight."

Adam listened to computer keys clicking. What would Jason find?

"Okay. Here we go. Assuming this is the same Tara James, which I can't guarantee without a date of birth, she was born in California, has a degree in library science, never been married. Lived most of her life in Palm Springs area."

"That's more than I knew. I owe you."

"And I'll collect. Now what?" Jason asked.

"You mean about Tara?"

"Yes."

"I guess I'll see where things go. I don't understand why she's so secretive about her past. But at least she didn't appear to have been in trouble with the law." Which was a huge relief. He half expected her to be on the run with outstanding warrants. He shook off the ridiculous thought. She'd never given any reason to think she was acquainted with the underbelly of society.

"None that I can find. She's squeaky clean. Not even a parking ticket."

"Okay."

"You don't sound happy. What gives?" This was why Jason was a good agent. He had a gut instinct that was rarely wrong.

"I'm happy," Adam said. "But I don't understand why she won't talk about her past if it's so innocent. Most people like to share antics from their childhood, but not Tara."

"Maybe she's a private person."

"Could be. Thanks again. If you're ever in Oregon, look me up."

"Will do. Same with you if you get up to Seattle."

"Sure thing." He disconnected the call and sighed. Jason had a good intuition about people that was always spot on, and he liked to think he did as well. Maybe he should come out and ask Tara about her past—there had to be a reason she was a ghost on social media. It was at least worth a try. After all, the worst that could happen is she could shut him down.

Chapter Six

Tara double-checked all the door locks and windows before heading to bed. The man from earlier today had seriously frightened her. She kept telling herself there was no reason to be afraid, but the tremors wouldn't stop.

Lord, please keep me safe and please give me Your peace.

Her doorbell rang. She stifled a scream. "Get it together, girl." She stood frozen in place. Should she answer it? The bell rang again. She tiptoed to the door then looked through the peephole. *Adam?* Her pounded even harder. She opened the door. "Hi. I thought you left hours ago."

"I did."

"But you're back."

"I am."

She grinned at his two word replies. "Would you care to come in?"

"I would." He stepped inside and closed the door. "You alone?"

Her heart tripped into double time. Had she made a mistake trusting him? "Why?"

"Just wondering if I interrupted."

"You didn't. Would you like something to drink? Tea, coffee, water?"

"No thanks." He followed her to the living room and settled onto the red chair she motioned to. It was her favorite for snuggling up in at night with a good book.

She sat on her white sofa with a red blanket draped over one arm. "Why are you here, Adam?" She looked around her small house and tried to see it through his eyes. The modern décor might look cold and uninviting to some, but to her it was ordered and gave her a sense of peace and harmony.

"I couldn't get you off my mind and needed to see with my own eyes that you're okay."

She shifted. "As you can see, I am." Having him here felt weird—not necessarily bad, but she wasn't accustomed to entertaining men. Who was she kidding? She never had guests.

"Yes."

She raised a brow. "But you're not convinced."

He shrugged. "You were pretty upset earlier today."

"I was, and I'm still creeped out. But I'll get over it. It's sweet of you to be so concerned." They'd hit it off for sure, but him stopping by again still seemed odd. Did he have an ulterior motive or was this typical for him?

His jaw set. "I know Carter asked this earlier, but do you have any reason to think that man wanted to harm you?"

She pushed down the wave of panic his question evoked. She'd thought Tipton would be safe, but it seemed nowhere was. "There've been several odd things happening in town this week, and I guess I'm jumpy." It might not be the complete story, but it was the truth. "I can't get baby Amelia out of my mind and then that poor woman who was struck and killed."

He winced.

"I forgot you knew her." Talk about the understatement of the century. From what he'd said they'd been very close at one time. Close enough he'd planned to propose. "I need tea." She stood, figuring he'd follow her to the kitchen. She'd bought coffee when she'd first moved in, assuming she would make friends who enjoyed it. But as it turned out she'd never acquired friends she felt comfortable inviting over, it was a good thing he hadn't wanted any because it was probably too old.

She busied herself filling the kettle with water then dropped a bag of chamomile and honey tea into her favorite cup. "Are you sure you wouldn't care for a cup of tea?" She glanced over her shoulder and frowned. He hadn't followed. "Adam?" She called. "Are you sure you wouldn't like a cup of tea?"

He popped around the corner. She screamed and slapped her hand to her mouth. Her heart raced and tears burned the back of her eyes. She needed to get a grip.

He rested a hand on her shoulder. "I didn't mean to startle you. I figured you'd hear me coming since you asked me a question."

He was right. She should have, but she was off today. She took a deep breath and let it out slowly, willing her pounding heart to slow. "Guess I'm a little jumpy. That man spooked me more than I care to admit."

He sat on a black barstool. "Why is that?"

She shrugged as she walked back over to her tea service area. She slid a metal box filled with an assortment of tea bags toward him. "Would you like to choose a flavor?"

He reached for one without looking and handed it to her. She tore off the wrapping and dropped it into her second favorite cup—all white with a black *fleur-de-lis*. At least he'd picked an herbal tea, so he wouldn't be awake all night.

The kettle whistled. She poured boiling water over the tea bags. "You asked why I'm jumpy."

Interest lit his face. He grasped his cup but didn't drink the tea.

"Something happened in my past. Ever since I've been..."

"On guard?"

Exactly. How was it he could put into two words how she'd felt for the past couple of years? "Yes."

"It's tough to let people in when you never let your guard down."

She brought her cup to her lips and sipped. He had no idea.

"I wish you'd trust me."

"Why?"

"Why should you trust me, or why do I wish you would?" He cradled the cup between his hands.

"Both."

"Because I care."

Was it really that simple? His face held sincerity.

"Thank you. That really means a lot. I feel like I can trust you, but some things are best left unspoken."

"Okay. If you ever change your mind..."

She dipped her chin. "I could use a friend."

"Funny, me too. How convenient." He grinned

then sipped his tea and made a face.

She laughed. "Not a tea drinker?"

He placed the cup onto the counter. "No."

"I could make you some coffee, but the bag is old."

He tsked. "That's almost criminal. I'll get you a bag of my favorite and teach you how to make it. Who knows, I might even convert you."

She laughed. "Not likely. But I'm game." A lightness she hadn't felt in a long time filled her. "Thank you."

"For what?"

"For making me laugh. It's been too long."

He reached for her hand and gave it a squeeze. "It's late. I should go home."

She walked him to the door and watched him drive away until she lost sight of his taillights. With a happy sigh, she turned. A scream ripped from her lips.

Nancy snuggled into Carter's side as they sat on her sofa. His nephew worked on homework in the kitchen. "I want a small wedding."

"Define small." Concern edged Carter's voice.

"Just our closest friends." A fairytale wedding had never been her dream. If she could, she'd skip the whole thing. She didn't understand why their wedding was so important to Carter. He had to be one of only a handful of men on the planet who felt this way. "I think we should keep our guest list below fifty."

"Sweetheart, you're the belle of this town. Do you have any idea how many people will be disappointed if they aren't invited to our wedding?"

"I'm not the belle, but you're right about a lot of people wanting to be there." She shrugged a shoulder. "I can't help wanting to keep it private. Maybe we could do a small ceremony then have a big reception after Christmas. We won't do a meal, just cake."

"That might work. All I know is a day doesn't go by that someone doesn't ask about our wedding and when they can expect their invitation."

She should have known they wouldn't get away with a small ceremony. She'd grown up in this town and knew most of the residents. "Do you realize we've been sitting here for an hour and have yet to make a concrete decision about our wedding other than Christmas Eve assuming we can get the church?"

"We could hire a wedding planner then you wouldn't have to deal with it at all other than to tell her what you want."

"You sound like Anna. She gave me the contact information for a woman she said was good. But what I really want is to elope." There. She'd said it. She tilted her head to have a better view of Carter's face.

"You tossed out the idea before, but I didn't realize that was what you really wanted."

"It is. I have my head full with trying to find Amelia's mom."

"Why is this any different than all the other cases you've worked on? You always manage to get the most out of life while solving your mysteries."

"This time we're talking about a precious baby. I

want so desperately to help her, but I feel like time is running out." Plus in the past, she'd only aided an investigation, she wasn't the sole person working the case. The pressure she felt was higher than ever, and she didn't want to let anyone down.

"Do you need help? I'm working the hit and run case, but I'm sure I could help you out if that will make a difference."

"It would, and yes, I'd love some information."

"Like what?"

She pursed her lips. "Something has been nagging at me since day one. It seems like too much of a coincidence that a woman was found dead on the side of the road not far from town on the same morning that an infant was abandoned at the library."

"You think the woman was the baby's mom?"

"It's crossed my mind."

"She's not. The medical examiner's report cleared that up right away."

She huffed out a breath. *Now what?*

"Sorry to disappoint you. It would have been a convenient answer for everyone, but that baby's mom is still out there."

"I want birth certificate records for live births in the past two weeks."

"I'll see what I can do about that. In the mean time, the local paper always posts baby announcements. Why not talk to Adam?"

"See, this is why I like working with you."

He chuckled. "You've sure changed since we first met."

"It so happens I enjoy bouncing ideas around with you."

He shifted. "I'm glad. But don't get too excited about the birth announcements. Amelia's mom might not be from around here."

"She has to be. Why else would she leave her baby at the library? A stranger driving through town wouldn't have done that."

"You never know. I need to get Gavin home. Morning comes too early. And Nancy?"

"Yes?" She sat up, missing the warmth of his body beside hers.

"I don't want to elope. Please let me know what I can do to help. I don't want you to be over burdened."

"Okay." But planning their wedding wouldn't stop her mind from working on the case. It'd be hours before she fell asleep. She'd call Anna, but her neighbor usually went to bed by nine. Tara crossed her mind. She'd never called on her employee for personal reasons, but Tara seemed very invested in this.

She stood and laced her fingers though Carter's as he strolled into the kitchen.

Gavin looked up from a book he was reading. "Time to go?"

"Yep." Carter pulled keys from his pocket. "You're driving. See you in the car."

Nancy walked out with him. Beside the driver's side door of his Charger, he pulled her into his arms and soundly kissed her. "Good night. Call me if you need any help with wedding plans or the baby case."

"I will."

Gavin jogged to the car and hopped in behind the wheel. She waved as they backed out. She went inside and pulled out her phone. It wouldn't hurt to call Tara. At the very least she could check on her and make sure she was doing okay. She'd been pretty shaken up this afternoon.

Chapter Seven

"WHO ARE YOU, AND WHAT ARE you doing in my house?" Tara reached for the pointy umbrella she kept hanging beside the door and held the point out like a weapon.

"Where is she?" The masked man asked.

"Who?"

"The baby."

"I don't know. DHS placed her somewhere."

The man cursed. "I want her."

"Then talk to DHS." There was no way that precious infant would be better off with this man than whomever she had been placed with. She prayed the social worker would protect Amelia from him.

He pulled out a small handgun and pointed it at her. "You're going to do that for me first thing tomorrow. I want an address."

Tara's grip tightened on the umbrella though it offered zero protection from a bullet. "What if they won't tell me?"

"Then you and I will have a problem."

She swallowed rising fear. *Lord, please send help.* "How will I get the address to you?"

"Leave it with Pepper at the coffee shop."

"*You* know Pepper?"

The man turned and fled out the back door. She raced after him, slamming the door and locking it behind him. At the door she peered out the window into the darkness, tossed the umbrella aside, and called 911.

"911. What's your emergency?" A calm female voice spoke into her ear.

"A man broke into my home and threatened me with a gun then ran off." She gave the operator her address and listened as the woman instructed her to get to a safe place. With trembling hands Tara re-locked the back door then headed to the front of her house. A siren sounded in the distance. She went to the window and watched for it as the sound grew louder by the second. A sheriff's vehicle rounded the corner to her neighborhood and stopped in front of her home.

"That was fast." She ended her call with the 911 operator and headed outside to meet the deputy.

A man who looked vaguely familiar approached her. The nametag on his shirt said Deputy Jacobson.

"He took off out the back door," Tara said. "I don't know which way he went."

The deputy spoke into a radio attached to his shirt alerting the other deputies about an armed and dangerous man. "Can you describe him, ma'am?"

"About five-foot-eight. A little pudgy in the waist. He wore a black ski mask so I didn't see his face." Her entire body shook. She needed to sit before her legs gave out.

"What else was he wearing?"

She closed her eyes trying to bring up his image in her mind and tilted to one side.

The deputy steadied her. "Why don't you sit?" He guided her to her front porch.

She sat on the top stair as he pulled out a small

notepad. She cleared her throat. "He wore faded jeans with a tear in the knee, work boots, and a black jacket."

He relayed the description to whomever he spoke to then returned his attention to her. "Do you know what he wanted?"

"Amelia. She's the baby that was abandoned at the library."

He nodded, clearly aware of the baby.

"He wants the address of where she's staying, and I'm supposed to give it to Pepper the owner of Roaster's Coffee." She gasped. "There was a man in there earlier today that gave me the creeps. Then he showed up at the library where I work but slipped away before the police showed up. I think he could be that same man who broke into my home, but I can't say for certain since he wore a mask tonight."

"You've had quite a day."

"Tell me about it." She hadn't had so much drama since...no she wouldn't go there. Dredging up that memory would only freak her out even more, and she needed her wits about her. "There's one more thing. He came in through the back door. It was locked, but there doesn't appear to be any damage to the lock."

"You think he had a key?"

"I don't know how, but yes. Unless he's an expert lock picker."

He frowned. "Do you have someplace else you could stay this evening?"

"You think he'll come back?"

The deputy shook his head. "Not likely, but it still would be a good idea to stay someplace else for the time being."

"I don't know where I'd go." Her phone rang. She checked the caller I.D. "It's my boss. That's odd. Excuse me a moment while I take this."

"I'm going to take a look around before I head out."

She nodded. At least her heart rate had slowed since the police officer arrived. "Hi, Nancy. I'm glad you called."

"Why's that?"

"I had an intruder in my home a little while ago, and the responding deputy suggested I stay someplace else tonight."

"Sweet juniper. Are you okay?" Concern filled Nancy's voice.

"He didn't hurt me. But I think if I don't give him what he wants he might."

"Pack a bag for a few days and come stay with me. Until this man is caught, you shouldn't be alone. I won't take no for an answer this time."

"It seems you take in strays more often than a shelter."

Nancy chuckled. "Only my friends."

"We're friends?" She pressed her lips together. She hadn't meant to say that out loud.

"I hope so. Now go pack. I'll be watching for you."

Tara pocketed her phone then raced inside her rented home. She grabbed her go-bag, which contained everything she'd need to disappear. Hopefully she wouldn't need it, but she didn't want to be without it. Then she packed another bag for her stay with Nancy. Hopefully, they'd have the guy in custody by morning, and she'd be able to come home.

Thirty minutes later, she parked in front of Nancy's house. The front door opened and Nancy stepped outside.

Tara left the go-bag in her trunk and instead grabbed her carryon-sized suitcase and wheeled it along the driveway to the front porch where her boss waited. "Thanks for taking me in."

"I'm happy to help. Let's get inside and warm up." Nancy ran her hands up and down her arms and led the way. "I put a kettle of water on to boil when I saw you drive up."

Her boss was a coffee drinker, but it appeared she was prepared for her guest's preferences. "Thank you. I'm really sorry to put you out."

"Don't be. I'm not put out in any way." She pointed to a door. "That's the guest room. Make yourself at home. I'll let you know when the water is ready."

"Thanks." Tara fled to the bedroom. Nancy had a heart of gold, but she wished she wasn't here. Staying with her boss was plain awkward. They worked well together, but had no relationship outside the library, which was fine by her. Getting close to a co-worker is what put her in her current situation. Ugh...she would *not* go there.

A few minutes later Nancy rapped softly on the doorframe. "Tea's ready."

"Thanks." She followed Nancy to the kitchen and sat on a barstool. "You never said why you phoned earlier?"

"I was calling to see how you were doing and to see if you were up to brainstorming with me. This baby case is driving me nuts. I have nothing."

"As it happens, I can help." She sipped the tea. "Chamomile?"

Nancy nodded and grabbed a piece of dark chocolate—her vice—from a small dish on the counter.

"It's good." Tara placed the mug onto the countertop. "The man who broke into my house wanted to know where Amelia is. He pulled a gun on me and demanded I get her address and deliver it to Pepper."

Nancy's eyes widened. "*My* Pepper? As in one of my closest friends." Nancy frowned. "We don't talk as much as we used to, but I don't believe for a second she has anything to do with Amelia."

"Whatever her connection is, this man is using her as a delivery mule."

"I should warn Pepper." Nancy pulled her phone out of her pocket. "She could be in danger."

"No. He's not going to hurt her. He needs her. Besides, Pepper has early mornings. She's probably been asleep for hours."

Nancy's movement stilled. "You're right." She worried her bottom lip. "Do *you* think Pepper is involved in some way? Maybe I'm too close to see what is right in front of me." She unwrapped another chocolate and dropped it into her mouth.

"I don't know her like you do. But if you say she couldn't be involved then that's good enough for me. Expect, she is involved because this dude is making her be."

Nancy tapped her fingernails on the counter. "Unless she has no idea. It's not uncommon for someone to give her a note and ask her to deliver it to a regular at her shop."

"That seems so archaic. With all the technology we have, why would anyone do that?"

Nancy shrugged. "There's something to be said for a handwritten note. Personally, I like that people around here are a little old fashioned."

"A little?" The town had virtually no nightlife, and it was old fashioned in so many ways. But that was what endeared Tipton to her. "I suppose I like it too, but it's still odd to use a handwritten note versus technology."

"Not really, Tara. He doesn't want you to know who he is. This method allows him to remain anonymous."

"True." Nancy was right. If she wasn't so distressed by everything going on in her life, she would have thought of it herself. She yawned. "It's been a long day. I should get some sleep."

"Of course. Rest well. If you need anything, just ask."

"I will and thanks. I don't know what I'd have done if you hadn't called." She probably would have stayed awake all night clutching that useless umbrella. She really needed a security system, but her landlord would never go for it. The man was as cheap as they came. She'd have to talk to him about the back door lock though. It shouldn't have been so easy for intruder to get in. It was almost as if he had a key, but that was impossible. Wasn't it? No, more than likely he was a pro at picking locks.

Early the next morning Nancy walked into Roaster's Coffee. Pepper stood behind the espresso machine. Nancy waited until the machine stopped making noise. "Hey there."

Pepper blinked. "You're early."

"I can wait if you need me to."

"It's fine. I'll get our donuts and coffee. I'm glad you're here. I could use a pick-me-up." Pepper grabbed a white mug and filled it with Nancy's favorite blend. "I'll plate the donuts and be right over."

Nancy settled into a seat at her usual table. The early morning crowd was quieter than when she normally came in.

Pepper placed a plate with a chocolate donut in front of Nancy then sat across from her with a scone and a hot drink. "What's going on to drag you from bed so early?"

"A man was in here yesterday."

"Lots of men come in here. What's so special about this one?" Pepper bit into her scone.

"He paid special attention to Tara and then he showed up at the library shortly thereafter. We also think he might have broken into her place last night."

Pepper gasped. "You're kidding."

"I wish. Did you ever get those surveillance cameras we talked about several months ago?"

"I have one on the entryway but that's it."

"Yes!" She ducked her head and held a hand over her mouth. "Can I see it?"

"Of course, but it records over itself every day."

"Why?"

"I didn't want to use up all the memory on my computer."

"You could store it in a cloud or external hard drive."

"Which costs money." Pepper looked annoyed by the suggestion.

"Sorry. I know it's a challenge to balance expenses." Now what? Deflated, she nibbled at her donut. She'd counted on that recording to show the identity of the man. If she could get a peek at him she was certain that she'd recognize him. Or at least be able to figure out his identity.

"What time of day were you hoping to see?" Pepper asked.

"Mid-morning I think." She gasped. "It hasn't been recorded over yet."

Pepper grinned. "Nope. Grab your grub and come to my office."

Nancy held the plate in one hand and her coffee cup in the other and followed Pepper. Excitement filled her. This was the break she needed.

Pepper sat at her desk and woke up her computer. The live feed played. "I'm not sure what to do."

"If you don't mind I can take over."

Pepper stood. "Go for it. I should get back to work. Let me know if you find what you're looking for."

"I will." She sped through the video until she found Tara and Adam then slowed it so she could see everyone who entered after them. She gasped when a man wearing a ball cap low over his eyes walked in. That must be him. She backed up the screen then froze it and took a picture with her phone. It wasn't super clear. It would have helped if he hadn't been wearing that hat, but it was better than nothing. She sent the photo to her mom then finished watching until he left. He did an excellent job of concealing his face.

Pepper popped into the office. "How's it going?"

"I think I found him."

"Excellent."

"Yes, but his face isn't visible." She held up the photo to Pepper. "I have reason to believe he will come in here everyday until he gets what he wants."

"What's that?"

"He told Tara to leave an address with you."

"With me?" Her voice squeaked. "Why?"

"I don't know exactly. I was hoping you would know."

Pepper shook her head. "I don't."

Nancy sighed. "Maybe he figures it's the safest way to stay anonymous."

Pepper's head jerked up and their eyes met. "You can't leave me here alone."

"You're never alone. There are always customers. It's the most popular place in town."

"Thanks, but I need *you*."

"I have a job."

"Let Tara run the library. You did it by yourself when she was gone, surely she can manage for a day."

"Maybe. But what if he notices me and gets spooked? Plus, Tara shouldn't be alone any longer than necessary."

"Please, Nancy. You're the brave one in this friendship."

Would Tara be willing to run the library on her own? Leaving her there alone was risky—Pepper would be fine considering the foot traffic this place received. Tara on the other hand would not be. "I have an idea." She shared her plan with Pepper.

"Genius. It's certain to work."

"I hope so." Nancy finished off the donut with two large bites then washed it down with her now cold coffee. "I'll be in touch." She stood and slipped out of the shop. If her plan worked, they'd know the identity of the man by day's end.

Chapter Eight

"YOU WANT ME TO WHAT?" TARA had maybe gotten an hour of sleep. Her head pounded, and her nerves were shot, but she'd come to work anyway. Now Nancy wanted her to take part in a scheme to catch the man who'd broken into her house. It was all too much.

Nancy sighed. "I want you to deliver a piece of paper with an address provided by the sheriff's department. The authorities will be waiting for him when he shows up."

The cobwebs finally cleared. "Oh. I suppose that could work. But what if he catches on to what we're doing?"

"He won't. The only people who know are Pepper—"

"You told Pepper? What if she's in on it with him? After all, he did tell me to give the note to her."

Nancy shook her head. "There's no way she's involved. If you had seen the look of fear in her eyes after I told her what was going on you'd have no doubt."

"Unless she's afraid because I told you. I could be in real danger. That man had a gun!"

Nancy put her finger to her lips. "Shh." She looked over her shoulder.

Tara crossed her arms. "No one is here."

Nancy rolled her eyes.

She never should have told Nancy what had happened. She should have done what the man said or packed up and left town last night. Instead she was stuck. There'd be no way she could leave now without him knowing. A chill ran through her. She hated being watched and could feel eyes on her. She whirled around and gasped. A man stood right outside the library and looked in through the glass door. "He's here," she said between her teeth. Actually, she wasn't certain that it was him. This guy seemed taller and younger, but no matter. He was a man, which to her way of thinking made him suspect.

Nancy stilled. She slid her hand into her pocket. "I'll have Carter drive by. Maybe if he sees the police he won't try anything. And you need to make a call—I mean *look* like you're making one. This is the perfect opportunity to make him think you're calling DHS."

Tara pulled out her phone and pretended to search for a number then acted like she spoke to someone. At least he wasn't inside so he couldn't hear that she wasn't actually talking. What if he had one of those listening devices? The kind that could be held by the person which transmitted everything someone was saying, even inside a building, without having a bug—she'd read about that in a book once. But wouldn't she be able to see it? No matter. She wasn't taking any chances.

She'd better make this look real. "Hi, this is Tara James. I'm the person who found an abandoned infant at the Tipton County Library." She paused for effect. "I was hoping to learn about Amelia and how she is doing." She paused again. "She is? Oh that's wonderful. I'd like to take her a gift. Would you be able to give me the address of where she's staying so I can drop it by?" She had no doubt it was against policy for them to give out addresses like this, but she hoped that the man watching didn't know. He needed to believe this ruse if he was actually listening.

She reached for a pen and pad of paper and pretended to write the address. "Thank you so much." She pocketed her phone and handed the pad to Nancy. "Do your thing."

Nancy shook her head. "He's still watching. Tear off the top sheet then walk into the stacks. I have the address on a piece of paper in my pocket. I'll put it inside a book." She turned her back on the entry and slid the paper into a book. She raised her voice. "Please add this book to the stack to be shelved."

"Sure thing, boss. Do you mind if I take an early break today? I'm meeting Adam at the coffee shop."

Surprise then approval filled Nancy's eyes. "Nice touch," she whispered. "Sure. I have a lot to keep me busy."

"Thanks. Can I get you anything while I'm there?"

"A black coffee."

"You got it. I have just enough time to shelve these books." More like call Adam and beg him to meet her. She had no idea if the man outside was actually listening, but she felt safer pretending he was.

She pushed the cart to the stacks then slid the paper with the address into her pocket and called Adam. "Hey, it's me. Something crazy happened. Can you to meet me at the coffee shop?"

"Okay," Adam said. "When?"

"Fifteen minutes?"

"See you there. Or I could stop by the library and we can walk together?"

Relief coursed through her. "I'd like that. Thank you."

"See you soon."

She pocketed her phone and worked as fast as possible to shelve the books. Nancy didn't really care if she finished before she left, but she would like to get them put back in their places. A moment later she heard a male voice. "That was fast." She strode from the stacks and froze. That wasn't Adam. In fact, she'd never seen this guy before.

"I was supposed to meet a woman out front about ten minutes ago, she hasn't showed. Did she perhaps come in here?" he asked Nancy.

"I'm sorry, sir. You're the first person we've had here today. Would you like to leave a note for her in case she shows up after you leave?"

He shook his head. "No thanks. I've tried texting and calling, but she's not responding. Guess I was stood up."

"If you don't mind me asking, who are you meeting?"

"Her name is Rachel Dillon. We've had this planned for a couple of weeks, but I haven't been able to reach her this week. I'm really concerned."

Nancy's eyes widened. "I'm so sorry to be the one to tell you, but Rachel is dead. Her body was found along the side of the road Monday morning."

His face blanched. "What happened?"

"You'll need to speak with someone at the sheriff's department. What's your name?"

"Kent Stevens. I'm her cousin. I was out of the

country until yesterday. I can't believe no one told me, although her ex-husband's an idiot, and I'm not close with my aunt and uncle so I shouldn't be surprised. This is horrible. Excuse me. I need to go talk with the police."

"They're located in the basement of the courthouse."

He nodded and rushed from the library.

Tara sucked in a breath. What a horrible way to find out about his cousin. Would Adam know Kent? She'd be sure to mention him. The books would keep. She traipsed over to Nancy. "That was awkward and really sad."

"I feel badly for him." A gloomy look rested on Nancy's face.

"Me too, but after everything that's happened, it makes me wonder if he was telling the truth about being her cousin."

"Why would he lie? He was obviously shocked by the news of her death."

Unless he was an exceptional actor, Nancy was right. She needed to stop being so suspicious of everyone. "Adam is meeting me here. We're walking to Roaster's Coffee together."

"Good idea. I wonder if he knows Kent?"

"I wondered the same thing. You can be sure I'll ask him."

The doors slid open and Adam strolled in. He grinned when he spotted Tara. "You ready?" He walked over to where she stood beside Nancy's desk. "Hi, Nancy."

She nodded. "Take good care of her."

He shot Tara a perplexed look. "Sure."

"I'm ready to go." Tara slipped into her jacket and felt for the slip of paper in her pocket. Her stomach filled with butterflies. This had better work. She strolled out with Adam, keeping on alert for any man who might be following them. "You'll never guess who stopped by looking for your old girlfriend."

His head whipped her direction. "Who?"

"Her cousin, Kent. Did you know him?"

"Sort of. They were close, but we've never met in person. I can't believe no one told him. But their family is kind of odd."

"Aren't all families?"

He chuckled. "Perhaps. What about yours?"

"Mine?" Her voice squeaked. "I suppose we're as unique as everyone else."

"But not odd?"

It had been a long while since she'd seen her family. Nancy thought she'd gone to visit them when she'd taken a leave of absence, but she used them as a cover story. In reality, she was lost to her family. It had to be that way for their own safety and hers. If anyone ever came looking for her, her family could honestly say they didn't know where she was. It needed to stay that way, but she sure missed them. Mom had always been her champion. She could count on her no matter what, but this time it was her turn to protect her mom. Her dad could spin a story that kept her on the edge of her seat every time. He was the best. She missed the sound of his deep, soothing voice.

"You okay?" Adam asked as he pulled open the door to the coffee shop.

She was so lost in her thoughts she hadn't

realized they'd arrived. "I've been better, but I'm hoping things will improve soon." They walked over to the counter together.

"Hi, Tara." Pepper brushed a crumb from the counter.

"Hey, there. I'd like mint tea for here, an extra hot coffee to go, and a pumpkin cream cheese scone. I'm paying for Adam's too."

"I can get my own." Adam pulled out his wallet.

"Nope. I told you last time, I'd get yours this go around." She raised a brow challenging him to argue.

He stuffed his wallet back into his pocket. "If you insist, but I'll get yours next time. I'd like a medium mocha please."

She reached into her pocket and pulled out the note along with a twenty-dollar bill. She made no secret of handing over the note. Hopefully the man, wherever he was, would notice. "Would you mind holding onto this note? Someone will be by later to get it."

"No problem."

They waited at the other end of the counter. A few minutes later they had everything and found a window seat.

"It's none of my business, but do you always leave notes here for people?"

She shook her head. "This is a first."

Adam cradled his coffee between his hands. "You mentioned that something crazy happened."

"Right." She lowered her voice and told him about her intruder, his demands, and why they were really there. The emotions that played across his face would have been comical if he hadn't looked so upset in the end.

"Are you in danger by being here?" He matched her hushed tone.

"I don't think so. He seems to only be interested in the baby. Since he wore a mask I can't identify him." Good thing too. She was tired of running. How was it that trouble always seemed to find her?

"I don't like it."

She hadn't told him about the address being a set up. That was need-to-know and he didn't need to know. "I'm not crazy about any of this, but it is what it is."

He reached across the table and grasped her hand. "You need to be careful. It's not safe for you to live alone."

"That's why I'm staying with Nancy until this goes away." She prayed she'd be back in her own place tonight.

"Good." He released her hand. "I don't want anything to happen to you."

"Thanks. Me neither." His concern warmed her from the inside out. "Tell me about yourself."

"Here? Now?"

"For a reporter, you sure have a way with words."

He chuckled. "I'm better with the written word. Do you need to get back to work?"

"Yes. I suppose it's time." She stood. "Let me get a tray for all of this." She'd eat the scone later. The door to the shop opened and a man walked it.

Was that him?

Chapter Nine

ADAM STARED AT THE COMPUTER SCREEN in his office after he left the coffee shop. He felt as though he'd stepped into an alternate universe. Life in Tipton had gone from somewhat boring to nutty in a matter of a week. Not to mention that he'd finally found a woman who interested him. He hoped the article he was about to send to his editor would light a fire under the local law enforcement. They still wouldn't discuss the details of Rachel's death. His gut said there was more to the story than what they had released to the public.

The door swung open, and a lean man who looked to be in his late twenties stepped inside.

Adam stood since he was the only person in the barebones office at the moment. "May I help you?"

"I'd like to submit a memorial piece for the Sunday paper's obituary section." The man handed him a piece of notebook paper.

"Submissions are normally done online." He looked down at the paper and spotted Rachel's name. He shot a look at the man. "An announcement was already made for Rachel."

"Who submitted it?"

"I did." He offered his hand. "I'm Adam Stacy. Rachel and I went way back."

A knowing looked filled the man's eyes as he shook Adam's hand. "It's good to finally meet you. I'm

Rachel's cousin, Kent. She used to talk about you but never said why you broke up."

"She never told me either."

Kent nodded. "She had a short attention span when it came to the men in her life. Did you know Rachel divorced her husband about six months ago?"

"No. We didn't keep in touch." Irritation flared. How dare he talk badly about Rachel? Then again, he was right. He'd give the man a break. If Rachel's best friend and cousin couldn't speak the truth then there was something really wrong with the world.

"About the memorial piece."

Adam looked down at the paper in his hand. "Right. Tell you what. I'll see what I can do. The editor won't run a second announcement, but maybe we can spin it in a different direction. Maybe it could be a human interest story."

Kent's eyes narrowed. "It's kind of short for something like that. What do you have in mind?"

"I could interview you about her childhood, her dreams, and hopes. Then submit it to the editor and see what he thinks. You interested?" This might be exactly what the public needed to get them passionate enough to start pressuring the sheriff's department to release more information about Rachel's death.

A tiny smile lifted Kent's lips. "I like how you think. I'm free now."

"Great." He motioned to a coffee pot on a table nearby. "Help yourself while I gather my thoughts." Rachel might have cheated on him and moved on without telling him, but she was still a human being and deserved justice. This piece might very well be the catalyst to that justice.

Five minutes later, he had a rough idea of the questions he'd ask. Kent sat beside his desk as Adam started his recorder. He'd learned a long time ago to record interviews so he wouldn't miss anything or misquote someone by mistake.

"I appreciate you taking time to do this. I'm sure you're busy. This paper looks like a one man show."

"It's my pleasure. There are three other reporters on staff along with the editor. We also take freelance articles."

"Sounds like a lot of work."

"We manage."

"I'm surprised you find enough to write about in a town this size."

Adam cleared his throat. "We should get started. What is the craziest thing Rachel ever did?"

"Rachel wasn't much of a prankster, but one day I talked her into helping me TP a friend's house." He chuckled. "We parked at the end of their long driveway and snuck in on foot."

Adam's eyes widened. He remembered this well. Everyone at school had talked about it. "She never said anything."

"You weren't dating yet. That experience emboldened her though. In fact, I think that's what gave her the courage to say yes when you asked her out."

"Seriously?" He'd never thought of Rachel as timid.

"Yes. That night empowered her."

"Interesting." He continued the interview, and before he realized it, an hour had passed and his editor was breathing down his neck. He quickly wrapped up the interview. "I'll let you know when or if this will go to print."

"Thanks." Kent shook his hand and left.

Adam turned to his editor. "I have an idea." He explained what he had in mind, and to his surprise, his editor immediately said yes.

"Send it as soon as it's finished. I'd like to add it to tomorrow's edition. It'll be our cover story."

Adam's pulse thrummed faster. The cover? He wasn't even sure he'd publish the piece much less have it on the cover. He attached headphones to his device and replayed the interview.

Two hours later he pressed send, releasing the story to his editor. He glanced at the clock—well past lunch. Time for a break. He'd finish his other article when he returned.

He shrugged into his jacket, grabbed his sack lunch and went outside. There was something about eating outside that invigorated him. A light drizzle fell from the clouds. He headed for his rainy day spot, not far from the library. Maybe Tara hadn't taken lunch yet. He shot off a text.

She immediately replied. *Can't get away.*

Disappointment filled him. He'd come to look forward to their daily visits even if he'd only known her a few days, but he'd seen her this morning for coffee. He shouldn't be so down. He sent another text. *Are you free for dinner tonight?*

Yes. When and where?

He grinned. *I'll pick you up at six.*

See you then.

"Yes!" He pumped his fist.

Nervous energy filled Tara. She had a date—the first in a very long time. When he'd asked the other day if she'd be interested in going out to dinner with him sometime she'd expected him to set something up right away and had been disappointed when he hadn't. But with all that had been going on it made sense that he'd wait a bit before scheduling it. She was just glad he had. What would she wear?

Nancy stood at the end of the stack where she was working. "I'm taking lunch. Will you be okay here alone?"

Tara dropped the book she had in her hand. "Umm. Do the police have that man in custody yet?"

Nancy shook her head. "I haven't heard a word, and I can't reach my mom. I suspect it might be going down right now."

"I sure hope so. I won't feel safe until he is off the streets."

"I understand. I'll order in for lunch today. Do you want anything?"

"I have a scone from Roasters."

Nancy wrinkled her nose. "You need more than a scone. I'll order a pizza."

"Greasy fingers and books are not a good fit."

"Point taken. Chinese it is. What would you like?"

"Orange chicken and fried rice." Nancy never ordered in food. In fact she was quite picky about food in the library. She must really be concerned.

"Sounds good. Think I'll get the same." She went back to her desk and placed the order. "I hope you're not too hungry. They said it'd be thirty minutes."

"That's fine."

Nancy's phone rang. She checked the caller ID then look excitedly toward Tara. "It's Pepper." She swiped the screen then put it on speaker. "Hi, Pepper, you're on speaker. Tara is with me."

"Good. A boy came in and asked for the note you left, Tara."

"A kid?" Disappointment filled her. "I expected the man who threatened me to pick it up."

Nancy shook her head. "He's not as stupid as we thought. He knows we'd be watching for him. The only person who can identify him now is the kid."

Tara gasped. "Is the kid okay?"

"I don't know. I assume so." Worry tinged Pepper's voice. "If he saw the man's face do you think...?"

"Let's pray not," Nancy said. "I'll let my mom know. Do you know who the kid was?"

"His name is Kai. He's a regular. He and his friends come in here almost every day after school."

"Oh. So we're not talking about a little kid." Nancy looked relieved.

"Sorry, no. I'm guessing Kai is about fifteen. He's a nice boy. Always respectful and throws his garbage away. I think he's on the wrestling team."

"Okay. Thanks for updating us," Nancy said.

"When you know something, please let me know."

"I will. We'll talk later." Nancy ended the call. "That was an unexpected twist."

Tara nibbled on her bottom lip. Would that teen be okay? She knew how crossing the path of the wrong person could mess up a life. She'd hate for his to be ruined or cut short. "What now?"

"I'll fill in my mom and then we wait."

Tara ran a hand through her hair. She couldn't take this stress, and all because some woman didn't have the sense to drop her baby off someplace legal.

Nancy rested a hand on her shoulder. "Are you okay?"

"No. I can't handle all of this drama."

"Why? You've always handled everything that's happened around here with aplomb. You were a cool cat when I discovered that snake under my desk."

"I know, but the snake was under *your* desk and wasn't meant for me."

"So as long as you're not the object of the threat, you're okay?"

"Pretty much." She sounded so selfish. "Don't misunderstand—I cared very much about the things that have happened to you, but I didn't feel threatened."

"And this time you do?" Nancy crossed her arms and leaned against the check-out desk.

"Yes. He broke into my house. Which incidentally, I have no clue how he did. There didn't appear to be any damage to the lock."

"Do you think he had a key?"

She nodded. "But I can't imagine how, unless he was a tenant there at some point. But I thought landlords had the locks changed when someone moved out."

"That would be the best practice, but there's no guarantee yours did. We need to find out for sure. If he did change them, then we need to figure out how he got in. I suppose he could have been an expert lock picker. If that's the case you might not be able to tell anyone picked it. Are you sure you had it secured?"

"Positive. I was going to go to bed early and distinctly remember checking all the door locks and windows." She had asked herself that repeatedly since last night and remembered checking it earlier in the evening. "And I'd already considered the lock picking idea. The more I think about it the more I believe that's what happened."

Nancy nodded. "I'm going to step outside for a bit while I make this call."

Tara forced a smile and nodded. Why didn't Nancy want her to hear that conversation? Did she know something she wasn't sharing?

After the library closed that evening, Nancy rushed to the sheriff's office. Her mom had texted to tell her they had the masked intruder in custody. Since the courthouse was only a couple of blocks away she walked—quickly. She wouldn't need her afternoon power walk with Anna today but would be sure to do it anyway. She needed to decompress with her friend. She stopped outside the door and took a calming breath before going in.

Lyle stood and walked toward her, his brow furrowed. "You shouldn't be here, Nancy."

"Why? This is my case." They'd tried to protect her in the past and even kept information from her, but it should be different this time—she was the lead on this since the department's resources were tied up investigating Rachel's death.

Lyle pulled her out into the hall. "You can't be seen here right now."

"But isn't the intruder in custody? I hoped to watch his interrogation."

Lyle shook his head. "Sorry, kiddo. When he broke into Tara's place and brandished a gun, everything changed. Your mom will call when she has more information. In the meantime, go home."

"But she's the one who called me. I thought she wanted me here."

Lyle's brows rose. "I was unaware. She's in her office." He escorted her to the sheriff's office. "Nancy wants to view the interrogation of our suspect."

Mom shook her head. "I'm sorry. I didn't mean to drag you over here. That text was so you and Tara wouldn't be worried about the intruder coming back. This guy is into some dangerous stuff, and I don't want either of you involved. I'm sorry. We need to go by the book. I want this guy behind bars for as long as the law allows and not have to release him on a technicality."

"Oh." Nancy frowned. This wasn't fair, but she understood. She certainly didn't want to compromise the case or put Tara in danger. "Fine. I'll do as you ask...this time," she teased.

"Thank you." Her mom's face softened. "Now get out of here before they move him to a holding cell and he sees you."

"I'm going."

Lyle escorted her to the exit. "I'm sure you'll stay in the loop, but at a safe distance."

"Okay. I'll see you." She still thought Lyle and

Mom belonged together, but they simply wouldn't cooperate, and Nancy had too much going on to try to play matchmaker. Those two would have to figure things out for themselves—hopefully they'd open their eyes someday to what she saw.

Carter strolled into the building. His brows rose. "Nancy. This is a surprise. I have a few things to wrap up before I leave. You want to wait?"

"Can't. I've been banished." She motioned toward the door Lyle had gone through only a moment ago. "They don't want me here."

"Because you could endanger yourself and Tara. I heard they'd caught the guy who broke into her place last night. Does Tara know?"

She shook her head. "Not yet—she left right before I got word of his arrest. I probably should've sent her a text to as soon as I knew, but I was hoping for more information first. I'll tell her when I get home."

"I imagine she'd want to know as soon as possible."

"Yeah." Maybe it would be best to text her now. She hadn't considered how stressed Tara was, knowing the guy was out there watching her.

She pulled out her phone and sent the text message. "She didn't say as much, but I know she's anxious to get back to her own place. Although she's great to work with, she doesn't appear to have any interest in being friends outside of work. Besides Adam that is, and he's new in her life. It's not like she has a ton of friends stopping by to see her. It's hard to believe they didn't know one another before this week. But he never came into the library, so I don't know how they would've met, now that I think about it. Anyway, they really clicked."

"Good for them. But I'm sorry she's not interested in being your friend."

Nancy pecked his cheek. "Thanks. I better go before I'm escorted from the building."

"Okay. Be careful, and watch your back."

"Why?"

He shrugged. "We don't know if the guy is working with someone else. Just be careful. Okay?"

"But I thought it was safe for Tara to return to her place."

"She's probably fine, but she should be—"

"Careful too. I get it. Can you come over tonight?"

"I need to see what Gavin's up to."

She nodded and left, still at little bummed they wouldn't give her any information or let her watch the interrogation. Ordinarily, she'd challenge Lyle or anyone else who tried to keep her from a case she was consulting on, but this was different. She would not do anything to put Tara in danger.

Rain fell as she exited the building. "How fitting." She raised the hood of her jacket over her head and walked back to the library. She should have driven.

A car pulled up alongside her and lowered the window. "Want a ride?" Anna asked from behind the wheel.

"Sure." She got into her friend's car. "Thanks. I'm parked near the library. I didn't expect it to be raining so hard."

"I think it took everyone by surprise. Do you mind skipping our walk today? Luke invited me over to his place, and I have some stuff to do first."

"No problem," she said her voice too chipper.

"You okay?"

"I'm a little down this evening. I'd hoped something I was working on would be wrapped up by now, but I learned I might be wrong."

Anna glanced her way. "Is this about the baby?"

"Not exactly."

"Then what?"

"I really shouldn't say." Nancy wanted to tell Anna everything, but Lyle's warning had her worried. She didn't want to drag Anna into anything that could get her hurt.

"You're not in any danger, are you?"

"I hope not, but it seems that whenever one deals with the underbelly of society that danger lurks nearby."

Anna chuckled. "Underbelly of society? What have you been reading?"

Nancy rolled her eyes. Pretty much everyone in her life said the vocabulary in the book she was reading would creep into her daily speech. Though she hated to admit it, they were right. "Just you never mind what I'm reading."

Anna huffed. "Fine. How are the wedding plans?"

"We're getting closer."

Anna pulled to a stop behind Nancy's '69 Mustang parked in front of the library. "If you need any help, let me know. It's been a while since I last planned a wedding, but there are some things you don't forget."

"Like riding a bike?" Nancy reached for the door handle. "Thanks. I might take you up on that. We agreed to keep it small, but there's a lot to do and not much time."

"Like I said, I'm happy to help."

"You're the best. Thanks, Anna." She got out and jogged to her car then stopped—something wasn't right. She peered at the back wheels. "You've got to be kidding me." Both back tires were flat. She squatted and found a puncture hole.

A car door closed and footsteps pounded on the asphalt. Anna squatted beside her. "Slashed?"

"Sort of. This is so frustrating. If someone has a problem with me, I wish they'd just say so rather than vandalize my baby."

"I completely understand. When my tires were slashed last spring, it was not only expensive, but I felt violated. What are you going to do?"

"Call a tow truck. I don't have two spares. At least I can wait inside the library."

Anna shook her head. "I'm so sick of stuff like this happening. I'm sorry about your tires."

"Thanks. You better go. You're getting soaked. Have fun tonight."

"I will. Call me anytime." Anna hurried to her car.

Nancy headed for the library. Carter's warning that the man in custody could have a partner niggled in the back of her mind. Feeling exposed, she hurried inside. This criminal made it personal when they messed with her car. No one did that and got away with it.

Chapter Ten

THE DELUGE OF RAIN FROM THIS afternoon had finally ended, and Adam couldn't be more pleased. Rain in Oregon this time of year was normal, but he had plans for an outdoor picnic. Maybe it was silly, but he really did enjoy eating alfresco. Hopefully, Tara did too.

He hummed an old 80s love song. He had strung white lights around his covered backyard gazebo this past summer and had enjoyed many evenings under the stars. He wanted their first official date to wow her and couldn't think of a more romantic setting, minus the rain. Good thing he'd added a portable propane heater this fall—they'd need it. The steaks were on the counter coming to room temperature and everything else was ready to go. Now all he needed was Tara.

He dashed inside and quickly changed into a sweater and a clean pair of jeans then headed out to pick up Tara. She'd sent him a text a short time ago with a different address from the one where he'd dropped her last night. Considering what had happened after he left, he was glad she wasn't there.

He pulled up in front of a house in a nicer neighborhood than Tara's and immediately spotted her standing on the front porch. She dashed to his car without giving him the opportunity to greet her properly.

She got in and closed the door. "I'm glad you saw my text about the address change. I was worried when you didn't reply."

"Sorry. I meant to, but I've been busy." He offered a smile, admiring her perfectly arranged blonde hair and long jacket that matched. Her ice blue eyes twinkled in the glow of a nearby street lamp.

"It's fine. Where are we going?"

"It's a surprise." He pulled out and headed toward his place. He couldn't wait to see her reaction to what he had planned.

"I'm not a fan of surprises."

He glanced her way. She didn't look happy anymore. "Don't be nervous. It's a good surprise. At least I hope you think so."

"Me too. I don't have a good track record with surprises."

"Do I make you anxious?" He frowned. He'd done nothing to make her feel uncomfortable around him. In fact, they'd hit if off from the moment they'd met.

"A little." She shifted and stared out the windshield.

"Why?" He'd observed her nervousness before but figured she'd grown more comfortable with him since she'd opened up some. What had caused this shift?

"I'm more comfortable with you than I am with almost anyone, but you have a mystique about you that makes me uneasy."

"And here I thought you'd enjoy a little mystery." His hands relaxed on the steering wheel. He liked that she thought he was mysterious even if it did make her a little uneasy. She'd get over it—at least he hoped she would. "Other than that, is everything else okay?"

"Not really. The police caught the man who broke into my house."

"But that's good news."

"Only partially. Someone vandalized Nancy's car today, and she thinks it's related because the police think the man who broke into my home wasn't working alone."

His grip tightened on the steering wheel. The case wasn't open and shut like he'd hoped. He shook his head. "I thought he wanted the baby."

"That's what he said."

"So what's he up to? Do they think this is some kind of baby ring?"

"I don't know, but I also have no idea what they're thinking. All I know is someone out there isn't happy, and they let Nancy know."

"Why Nancy?"

"Great question. Maybe because she took me in last night. Or maybe it's because she works at the library too."

His jaw clenched. "Interesting theory. Nancy sure knows how to find trouble."

"That she does. But in all fairness, this was quite literally dropped on her doorstep."

"Right." There was a story here, and he aimed to discover the truth behind what was going on. He parked in his driveway.

"Where are we?"

"My house," he said. "I hope you don't mind a home-cooked meal."

She hesitated.

Uh-oh. Had he over-stepped? Maybe coming to

his place made her uncomfortable. "I heard that new Italian restaurant is pretty good if you'd prefer going out."

"Not at all." She reached for the door. "A home-cooked meal sounds nice."

He was going for great or stupendous, but he'd take nice. "Allow me." He strode to the passenger side of the car then pulled open her door. "I thought we'd grill steaks."

"Sounds delicious." She walked beside him.

He opened the door. "After you."

"Thanks." She shrugged off her coat.

He caught his breath. "You look amazing." Her black dress skimmed her curves and hit just above her knees. "I hope you won't be cold though. I'd planned for us to eat outside." He motioned toward the rear of his house.

She cast a hesitant look toward the French doors that led to his backyard.

"I have an outdoor heater and fireplace to help keep us warm and the gazebo is covered. With your coat and a blanket for your legs, I'm sure you'll be fine," he quickly added.

"Your backyard is lovely—magical," she said with awe. "You must enjoy spending a lot of time outdoors."

He followed her gaze and took in the lit gazebo and planters. "Very much." He had spent countless hours turning his backyard into his own version of paradise. "Thanks. Shall we?" He strode to the kitchen.

He put the steaks on the grill while she helped set the food on the table. The steaks sizzled and the aroma made his mouth water. A short while later they sat at the round wooden table in his gazebo. Tara looked in awe at the spread. Satisfaction filled him. He bowed his head and offered a silent blessing for the food. When he looked up, Tara was doing the same. He grinned and waited for her to finish. "Dig in."

"Are you a cook on the side?" She filled one half of her plate with green salad.

"It's a hobby." He shrugged. "I like to eat." When he struck out on his own after college, he'd quickly realized he needed to up his game in the kitchen. Inspired by the cooking shows on television, he'd taken a few cooking classes and now felt comfortable there.

She chuckled. "Same, but I'm not the greatest cook." She placed the steak on the other half of her plate then cut off a piece and took a bite.

He held his breath, hoping it tasted a good as it looked.

"Mmm. You really do have talent. If journalism doesn't work out, you could cater backyard parties."

He released his breath, and his shoulders relaxed. "Nah. I'm fortunate to have the time and resources to indulge in my passions, but I'm not interested in making it a job. I think it'd lose the appeal."

"I can see that. What else do you do?" She speared another slice of steak.

"Not much. The paper consumes much of my time, and working in the yard relaxes me."

"I'm impressed."

"Thanks. What about you?"

"Not much to tell. I'm boring. I live in a rental, so I'm not investing in the yard, and cooking isn't my favorite thing to do."

"I didn't expect you to have the same hobbies as me. Don't you enjoy anything outside of work?" She didn't strike him as a workaholic.

"Sudoku and reading."

He laughed. "I suppose that makes sense, considering you work in a library. But Sudoku surprises me."

She ducked her chin. "I like numbers."

Was she blushing? It was difficult to tell in this lighting. "What else do you enjoy?"

"I don't know. Movies I guess."

"What's your favorite movie?"

"You'll laugh."

"Maybe."

A twinkle lit her eyes. "*Robin Hood*."

"Which version?"

"The cartoon." She plopped another bite of steak into her mouth.

He laughed. "Sorry. I'm really not laughing at the movie but rather the way you said it with such ease as if adults watch cartoons all the time. What is it about that movie you enjoy so much?" He firmly believed a person's favorite movie told a lot about them.

"I enjoy the interaction of the characters. They make me smile. I like that good prevails over evil, and those foxes are so cute."

He grinned. She had a romantic side that wanted justice to prevail. He liked that very much. "What else?"

"I don't know. What about you? Favorite movie?"

"I have more than one. But I think *Field of Dreams* and the original *Star Wars* movie tops the list." He grinned. "At least for right now."

"Why?" She rested her elbows on the table, interlacing her fingers.

"*Field of Dreams* is filled with hope. Anything is possible." He needed to believe that anything was possible. It's what drove him.

"I like that. I wish in real life anything was possible."

"Anything *is* possible."

She shook her head. "You're a dreamer, Adam."

"Maybe, but I also believe anything is possible with God."

"I see where you're going with this now. Okay, I'll give you that. But He doesn't always deliver."

"Such as?"

"Take Amelia for instance. That baby was abandoned, and now some gun-waving dude wants to know where she is. Her mom left her outside the library, presumably with the hope she'd have a better life. What kind of life will she have with a start like that?"

"It's not how you start, it's how you finish."

"I've heard that before. Maybe you're right." She eased back against the chair with a contemplative look on her face.

"Are you finished eating?" He asked. She had devoured her steak but only ate a few bites of her salad. "I have homemade ice cream in the freezer for dessert."

"My favorite. What flavor?"

"Lemon basil."

She made a face. "Think I'll finish my salad."

He chuckled. "Don't knock it until you try it. It's delicious, even on a cool fall evening."

She focused on her salad so he did the same. They'd talked so much he'd neglected his too. A short while later they stacked everything onto a tray, and he carried it into the house. "Want to grab the ice cream from the freezer while I clean this up. It will need to thaw a little while before we can dig in."

"Sounds good." Tara took the ice cream out of the freezer and placed it on the counter then moved to help Adam with the dishes. He wasn't what she expected yet in a way she wasn't surprised. He truly was a man of surprises. And shockingly, she wasn't put off by that characteristic.

"Who taught you to cook?" When they set up this date the last thing she'd expected was that he'd cook, let alone that it'd be delicious.

"I took some classes after college." He shrugged. "Like I said, I like to eat."

She chuckled. "Me too, but taking a class or two never crossed my mind. I wonder if there is one offered in Tipton."

"It's worth looking into, but I haven't heard of any. You could always enroll in one in Salem. That's where I went."

She nodded. "Care to take one with me?"

His brow furrowed.

"Not as a date or anything, just as friends," she

quickly added. Not that she wouldn't mind being more than friends, but her life was too complicated for more than that. Besides, she'd never go alone, especially now. As much as she liked Adam, what she really needed was a friend.

"If it works with my schedule. Do some research and let me know." He tilted his head her way. Even with suds halfway up to his elbows, he was handsome. She liked a man who knew his way around a kitchen and didn't mind cleaning up after himself.

What was she doing? She was falling hard and fast for him and she couldn't. She needed to be free of entanglements. A casual date and friendship was one thing, but if things went south, she didn't want to break his heart or hers by disappearing again—unless he'd be willing to go on the run with her. But she could never ask him to do that.

"You okay?" A concerned look covered Adam's face as he pulled the water stopper from the sink and placed it on the counter.

"I'm fine. My mind wandered. You think the ice cream is thawed enough to scoop?" Not that she really wanted any. She was still full, and it didn't sound all that appetizing. Then again, everything else he'd made was perfect so she ought to give the ice cream a chance.

He grabbed an ice cream scoop and dug into the creamy looking treat. "One scoop or two?"

"One, please. Are you going to the harvest festival next month?"

"Never miss it. How about you?" He handed her a bowl of ice cream.

"Yes. The library has a booth. We sell shelf-worn books to raise funds for our summer reading program." She took a tentative bite then smiled and took another.

"I remember. So you'll be working the booth?"

"Off and on. Volunteers will help, but Nancy or I should be there."

"I imagine it helps that it's only on a Friday evening rather than all day on Saturday."

"Yes, that does make it easier." Her phone vibrated indicating an incoming text message. She pulled out her phone.

Where are you? The icon flashed as Nancy appeared to be typing more.

At Adam's house. She replied.

Okay. A sheriff's deputy is on his way over.

"Everything okay?" Adam asked.

"I'm not sure." She held out her phone for him to read the message.

"Hmm. Another message popped in."

She turned the screen so she could read it.

The authorities have reason to believe you're in danger. The deputy will make sure you stay safe.

Tara clamped her teeth together. It was time to leave. Again.

Chapter Eleven

TARA GLARED AT NANCY AND ADAM who were planted in front of her, blocking Nancy's driveway. "Let me pass."

"Not until you tell me why you refused protection," Nancy said.

Tara's car sat only feet away with her go-bag, and they stood between it and her escape. Her entire body shook. Her knees actually wobbled to the point if they didn't move soon she'd be sprawled on the grass. "Please, Nancy. I don't want to fight you over this." She looked at Adam. "Or you either. There are things neither of you know."

"Then enlighten us, and explain why you won't accept protection." Nancy crossed her arms and had a look on her face she'd never seen before.

"I know you're only doing this because you care, but I'm not telling you because I care about you too."

"That makes no sense," Nancy said.

"Please, Nancy. I don't have a lot of time."

"Then start talking."

She blinked back tears of frustration. "Fine. You asked for it. But don't hold me responsible if you end up dead at the bottom of some lake."

"Hyperbole," Adam said. "It can't possibly be that bad."

Of course, he'd think that. She sighed. "I'm not exaggerating." The only way she was leaving here was if she told the only two people she truly cared about in this town about what happened, thereby putting them in mortal danger. "I've never told anyone this. In fact, I try not to think about what happened. It's serious. My family doesn't even know where I am. If they knew they'd be in danger. Are you sure you want to know?"

Adam and Nancy nodded in unison without hesitation. It figured. Her sleuth boss never backed down from danger, and Adam had busybody in his DNA.

"Three years ago, a co-worker I was dating became involved with a crime syndicate who smuggled drugs from South America. I accidently walked in on a meeting and saw key people along with a ton of cocaine. I didn't realize at first what was going on because my co-worker rushed me out of there so fast. He told me to forget what I saw, gave me a brief rundown of what I'd walked in on since I refused to leave, then he gave me a wad of money and said to disappear."

"He trusted you," Adam said.

"I guess he did." She hadn't thought about that. "I wasn't going to take the money until I saw two thugs with big guns come outside after me. I grabbed the money and ran. By the grace of God I got away and never stopped running until I landed here. I've never heard from him again."

Adam shook his head. "He's probably dead since he helped you."

Tara sucked in a breath. She had mulled over that scenario at least a hundred times but had been afraid to try and find him online in case the bad guys were watching for her. She didn't want to think he'd died saving her, but it was time to face the truth. Patrick was more than likely dead because she'd followed him to that warehouse. They'd dated for close to a year. In the final months he'd changed. She'd thought he'd been cheating on her and wanted to see for herself where he went when they weren't together.

She should have known better. Her parents said he was trouble. How had they known? The man she saw at work was courteous, professional, always finished his tasks on time. He was the ideal employee. The ideal man. Maybe he was too perfect—that should have clued her in. No one was that perfect.

Now she lived a life of regret and what-ifs. What if she hadn't followed him that night? What if she hadn't said yes when he'd asked her to dinner? What if...a sob escaped. "I'm so sorry. Now you know, and your lives could be in danger too. If they find out that I was here, they'll find out that I was close to the two of you and think you know where I am. My worst fear is someone I'm close to being tortured for information about me."

"What about your family?"

"I have a PI on retainer, keeping an eye on them. So far they're fine. My guess is as long as I stay away they'll be safe."

Adam ran a hand along the back of his neck. "You need to let the police help you. Tell them what you know."

"No way! I'm alive because I kept my mouth shut."

Nancy had paled. "There's something else."

"What?" Tara asked.

"The police kept this from you, but I think you need to know. Amelia's car seat had a large amount of drugs stashed in it."

"What?" Could it be connected to the syndicate in Florida? Oregon was a long way from Florida but who knew how far their tentacles stretched. Could she ever truly escape the cartel and live free from fear? Was anyplace on earth safe?

Nancy's heart pounded as she stood on the sidewalk outside her house. Tara and Adam stood silently as if waiting for her to tell them what to do. She enjoyed solving mysteries, but Tara's secret was not what she'd expected. What should they do? Her mom and Carter would know how to keep Tara protected, but they were cops. The only safe way they could help would be not using the law enforcement tools they had at their disposal. No checking online or talking to anyone. "We need to go inside."

Tara shook her head vehemently. "No way. I'm leaving."

Adam took her arm. "You need help. Let us help you."

She yanked free. "I told you why I have to leave. You're in danger as long as I'm here."

Nancy shot Adam a look telling him to back off. Hopefully, he caught it. "I understand your fear and that you're afraid for us." She hesitated. There was no going back if she stepped into this. Assisting Tara was the right thing to do. "But I'm in a position to help you where no one else could. Do you really want to be looking over your shoulder for the rest of your life? Never able to settle down and have a life?"

Tara's eyes watered. "Of course I don't want a life like that. But it is what it is."

"It doesn't have to be," Nancy said gently. "Let us help you."

Tara's gaze locked onto Adam's. "Why are you doing this?"

"We care," Adam said. "I don't want to lose you. Please, Tara." Adam's eyes pleaded with her.

If Nancy hadn't been watching so closely she'd have missed Tara's slight nod. She blew out a breath. "Okay. We need to get inside. Now." She looked from side to side as they rushed indoors. No one appeared to be paying them any special attention.

Tara wrung her hands and paced Nancy's living room. "Now what? We can't just sit here and wait for them to find me."

"I'm thinking," Nancy said.

Adam snapped his fingers. "I could get my FBI contact to help us."

"No!" Tara and Nancy both said in unison.

He crossed his arms. "Why not?"

"Because he'd have to open an official investigation," Nancy said.

"So?"

"So, if there is even one dirty agent there or if he innocently says something to someone who says something to someone else it could get back to the wrong person. I'd be dead and so would you and your friend." Tara plopped onto the couch. "This is hopeless. There's nothing anyone can do to help me."

Adam eased down beside her. "Hold on. You're not only assuming the worst, but you're giving up without even trying."

"Assuming the guys I walked in on in Florida have something to do with Amelia, then the longer I stay here the more we're all in danger. I should leave. It's too much of a risk." She leaned forward to stand.

Adam placed a hand on her knee. "Give us one day to come up with a plan."

Tara shook her head. "No way. That's too long. You have one hour."

Nancy's jaw clenched. "Fine. You and Adam stay here. I'll be back."

"Where are you going?" Adam asked.

"Never mind. Keep our girl safe." Nancy thought about the handgun in her nightstand. But decided against telling them about it. So far no one had directly threatened Tara. Her slashed tires could have been random, but it could also be connected. Either way whoever was behind it needed to be stopped.

Nancy made a call and learned her mom was still at work. She could have had this conversation over the phone but didn't want to risk anyone listening in since neither of their lines were secure. She strode into the Tipton County Courthouse and made her way to the sheriff's department. The door opened as she approached, and Lyle walked out. "Don't stop me. I need to see Mom. It's important."

Lyle frowned. "What's wrong?"

"Is she still in her office?"

He nodded.

"Thanks." She hurried inside and went straight to her mother, relieved to see she was alone. Nancy closed the door then the blinds on the window facing the inner office so no one could see in. "You're here late."

"Busy day." Her mom sat back in her chair, brows raised. "This is a first. What's going on?"

"Any chance your office is bugged?"

Her eyes widened. "No one would dare." She held up a finger then began a visual sweep of her office. Nancy got down on her hands and knees to look and feel under the furniture for a listening device. Satisfied no one was listening, Nancy sat and powered off her phone out of extreme caution.

Mom sat tall behind her desk. "Care to tell me what this is all about?"

Nancy told her everything. "We have..." she looked at her watch, "twenty minutes to come up with a plan or Tara bolts."

"That explains a few things. Let me make a few calls."

She shook her head. "No one can know. It's too dangerous."

"What do you propose we do?" Annoyance rested on her mom's face.

"I say we draw out the bad guy and arrest him."

"It's not that easy. If this is a crime syndicate like you suggest, then this is bigger than one person—a person, I might add, who is more than likely a patsy."

"Then what do we do?" Frustration seeped through to Nancy's core. She told Tara they'd help. She'd prevented her from escaping. If something happened to Tara now it would be her fault. She couldn't have Tara's life on her head.

"You let me do my job my way."

“But—”

“Nancy!”

She pressed her lips together. Mom never raised her voice.

“If you want to help your friend, then you need to trust me.” Her mom stared her down.

“I do. But Tara won’t stick around without a plan.” Nancy squirmed in her seat.

“I can arrange for a safe house.”

“In the movies the bad guys always find them.” Nancy crossed her arms.

“This isn’t the movies and this house isn’t official. No one but me knows about it. Satisfied?”

Nancy uncrossed her arms. “Okay. What’s the plan?”

“Need to know.” The sheriff’s jaw jutted.

She wasn’t talking to her mother anymore. Sheriff Daley had taken over, and Nancy would get nowhere with her now.

“Go home. I’ll be in touch. The code word is *sweet junipers.*”

Nancy grinned.

“If anyone knocks on your door and doesn’t say the code you don’t answer. Got it?”

“Yes, ma’am.”

“Good. Now go before Tara flees and gets herself killed. One dead body to deal with this week is more than enough.”

Adam held Tara’s trembling hand as they sat side-by-side on Nancy’s couch and listened for her to return.

"I need to confess something."

"Uh-oh. What?"

"I contacted my buddy with the FBI last night." The words rushed from his mouth. His neck burned.

"Why?" Panic filled her voice.

"I was curious. Something about you didn't add up." Clearly his instincts were on target, but had he made things worse? He trusted Jason, but could Jason's search have tipped someone off about Tara. "Is Tara James your real name?"

She shook her head. "Not exactly. I knew someone by that name in college. We became friends because our names were so similar. My first name is Beverly. My middle is Tara. We have the same last name. She was a lit major, and when I saw the job opening online for the library, I was inspired."

"You stole her identity?"

"No. Only some of the facts from her life. I'm still using my own social security number. But my first name is how everyone from my past knew me so I figured I'd be safe. I used Tara's backstory as my own when I came to Tipton. Even claimed to be from California on my rental application."

"If whoever those people were in Florida tried hard enough, they could find you with your social security number." Adam frowned. She hadn't broken the law, but she had been deceitful to get her job. Under the circumstances, he understood. "What is your degree in?"

"Accounting."

He chuckled. "Nice. So if I ever need help with my taxes, I know where to go to."

She winced. "Am I a horrible person?"

"No. You have good survival instincts. If anything, you could have done a better job. Using your own social security number was risky."

"I know, but I'm not a law breaker."

That rang true from everything he knew about Tara, or rather, Beverly. "Do you miss being called Beverly?"

She shrugged. "It took some getting used to, but it's fine now." She glanced at her watch. "Nancy is taking forever." She stood and paced the room. "What if she—"

The door burst open.

Tara yelped.

Chapter Twelve

TARA'S GAZE SHOT TO THE FRONT door where Nancy had burst in and slammed it behind herself, locking it and putting a finger to her mouth. Tara's heart pounded. Adam moved to her side and placed a reassuring hand on her back.

"Do we have a plan?" Adam asked.

Nancy nodded. "We wait for my mom. She has a safe house for you that no one knows about except her. I'm guessing we'll smuggle you out of here and get you there under the cover of darkness. By morning you'll have disappeared and whoever is behind this will be none the wiser."

Tara should feel relieved, but tension still knotted her neck and shoulders. This was good news. She would finally be safe. So why was she still terrified? "Will I be there alone?" She did not want to be hiding out alone, but at the same time, if someone came with her, they were at risk. No matter what, this plan stunk.

"I don't know. Mom is working on the details. If I could, I would go with you, but if neither of us show up at work Monday morning it will draw way too much attention."

"No. You need to go on with your life like normal." She understood why Nancy couldn't stay with her and honestly didn't expect her to.

"I'll tell anyone who asks that you're under the

weather."

That was definitely the truth. If she had a do-over in life, she would never have dated Patrick. For that matter, she would have never taken that job. She sensed something was off there but figured it was her overactive imagination. Was the entire firm on the take? She shook her head at the direction her thoughts had taken her. Patrick had been a good guy when she'd met him—at least she'd thought he was. It was only later he got into trouble. It had nothing to do with their place of employment.

Adam gently took her hand and tugged her back to the couch. She shook away her musings and sat beside him. "It's going to be okay." He rubbed her cold hands between his.

"How do you know?" She hated it when people assumed everything would be okay for no good reason.

"I suppose I don't, but I have to believe it will be, because in a very short amount of time I've come to care a lot about you."

She sucked in a breath. He felt their connection too—she'd tried to deny it but now that he'd acknowledged his feelings, she couldn't. She should have guessed he was interested in her since he'd invited her to dinner, but she was out of practice with dating and men in general. But how could they move forward?

Nancy brought them each a cup of tea. "I only have an herbal mint. I hope it's okay."

Tara dragged her gaze away from Adam's. His confession rocked her to her core—it complicated things to say the least. "How thoughtful. Thank you."

Tara sipped the brew and let it warm her as it slid down her throat. "It's good."

A knocked sounded on the door. Tara bolted to her feet, sloshing her tea. She shook away the burning sensation and placed the cup on a coaster.

Nancy put a finger to her mouth and motioned Tara to get out of sight. "Who is it?"

"Mom."

"I'm a little busy. Can you come back later?"

"Sweet juniper, girl," the sheriff said.

Nancy grinned, blew out a breath, and opened the door.

The sheriff stepped inside. "Well done."

Nancy crossed her arms. "You were testing me?"

"Of course. You passed. Now where's our girl?"

Tara stood. Her pulse still thrummed in her ears. She was sure to age ten years from all of this. "Right here." She glanced toward Adam. Would she ever see him again? She dearly hoped so, but she knew how things worked and didn't hold out much hope. Why did she have to meet him now, right when her world was falling apart? Again.

"Good." The sheriff raised a bag and handed it to Tara. "Put this on and hurry. I want to get you out of here ASAP."

Tara looked inside the bag and then back at the sheriff. "A wig?"

"Yes, along with a cap to tuck your hair into. It was the closest I could find to Nancy's hair. You're going to dress up like her, and if anyone is watching, they'll think we are heading out."

"You don't think they'll know it's me?" She looked at the bag skeptically. They were roughly the same size and build—very roughly, Nancy had a larger build. It's be a tough sell to get anyone to believe she was Nancy.

"I'm counting on the darkness to aid in our subterfuge. Now hurry."

Nancy moved forward. "Come on. I'll help. You can borrow one of my jackets too."

Tara's stomach churned. "Do you think this will work?"

"I do. Mom is great at what she does. You can trust her."

Tara nodded. She was trusting the woman with her life, because it was probably too late now to escape this small town without alerting whomever was after her that she was on the move.

Nancy held out the wig and skullcap or whatever it was called. "Go ahead and put it on then I'll arrange it so it looks like mine."

Tara fitted the cap over her head, making sure all her hair was tucked inside then tugged the long chestnut-colored wig into place. She stared at herself in the mirror. "Not bad. I haven't had long hair since before I was on the run. I forgot how much I like it."

Nancy fingered strands into place. "When this is all over you can grow your hair however you'd like. Are you a natural blonde?"

"Yes. I come from a long line of blonds. It was dyed it when I first came to town. I'm so glad I finally felt comfortable to go back to my natural color."

"Me too. It's perfect on you. I'm surprised you dyed it to begin with."

She cringed. "Cutting it was hard enough, but I really had no choice." Her long hair had been her pride and joy. Seeing her locks on the bathroom floor had been painful, but necessary. Since then she'd found a style she enjoyed so it wasn't so bad anymore.

"I suppose no matter what you did, it was inevitable they'd find you unless you went off grid."

"You're probably right." A commotion coming from the living room drew her attention. "What do you think is going on?" Her eyes met Nancy's in the bathroom mirror.

"It sounds like Adam and my mom are having a disagreement. We'd better get in there." Nancy did an about-face and rushed toward her living room.

With a fleeting glance in the mirror, Tara raced after her.

Adam stood with his fists at his waist, legs in a wide stance, and his chin jutted out. "You can't leave her there alone. Let me come."

Sheriff Daley shook her head. "People will notice if you don't show up for work on Monday."

"No, they won't. I can work from my computer. I'm doing a series on the hit and run and the Sheriff's Department."

Her mom's brow furrowed. "About that. I would really appreciate it if you'd stop stirring up the community."

"The public deserves answers."

"And they will get them as soon as I'm ready to release the details. There's more going on than you know."

"Then tell me."

"No."

Tara cleared her throat. "Excuse me, but I

wouldn't mind Adam's company. Who knows how long it will take to catch this guy and take down his organization?"

Sheriff Daley's face softened. "I know this is difficult, Tara, but it's for the best if only I know where you are."

Tara sucked in her bottom lip, took in a breath, then let it out. "Understood, but since it's my life, shouldn't I have a say?"

"You're making my job more difficult." The sheriff blew out a breath. "Fine. If this is what you truly want, then I'll figure out how to get Adam there without drawing undue attention."

The sheriff raised a brow at Adam. "I don't suppose you have a bag with you?"

"I keep one in my car. I never know when a story will break, and I'll be on the move."

"Okay. You leave first. We'll meet you at the state park outside of town."

Adam shot a triumphant look at Tara. "See you soon."

Tara's heart pounded. He really cared. For the first time in a long time she felt...loved. Her eyes widened. Love? It was too soon for that. He was being a good friend that was all.

While the sheriff walked him out, Nancy handed Tara one of her coats and a phone.

"What's this for? I have a phone."

"Leave it here. It's traceable. This is a burner. Only use it in case of an emergency."

Tara swallowed the lump that had formed in her throat. "If I don't see you again, please know how much I appreciate everything you've done for me."

"Don't think like that. You're going to see me again, but before you leave, I have one question."

"What's that?"

"Remember when you left town for about a month? You said you were visiting your sick mother. Clearly that wasn't the truth. Where did you go?"

"I thought I recognized someone that looked like one of the cronies that Patrick worked with in Florida. It took a while, but the PI I employ determined I was mistaken and said it was safe to return."

Nancy nodded. "I see. But where did you go?"

"California. It's pretty easy to disappear down there. I thought about staying for good, but I much preferred my life here, in spite of the rain."

The sheriff popped her head inside the doorway. "You ready?"

"Yes." She hugged Nancy then shut off the lights and pretended to lock up so if anyone was watching they would believe it was Nancy heading out. She walked silently beside the sheriff and slipped into the front seat of her personal car. "Thanks for helping me," Tara said.

"It's my job."

"Maybe, but it feels personal."

"The place we're going is rough. It's an old hunting cabin my ex-husband used to stay at. I won it in the divorce."

"How long since you were last there? Is it habitable?" Tara recalled that Nancy had once mentioned her dad had left them when she was a child.

"It's maintained as a rental. The renters who were scheduled to arrive yesterday were no shows."

"What if they plan to come in later?" Tara asked.

"It's been taken care of. The place is yours for the remainder of the week."

"Then what?"

"One step at a time."

Fear consumed Tara. If the woman she was putting her faith in didn't know what was next, what hope did she have?

Adam stood right inside the entrance to the cabin with Tara beside him. It opened directly into the living space. A small kitchen and a peninsula with several stools took up the far wall on the left. A ladder accessed a loft above the back half of the cabin. Two sets of bunk beds occupied the loft.

Sheriff Daley sauntered to the kitchen and placed two bags of groceries on the counter. She pulled open the fridge. "I asked the rental company to stock the fridge with necessities. I'm glad to see they did it." She turned to face them. "It's not much, but it has the important stuff—fresh fruit and vegetables and some meat to get you through the week. The restroom is behind that door." She pointed to the right. "I'll be back in a few days to check on you."

Tara stepped forward. "Thank you for doing this. I don't know how I can ever repay you."

"Just stay safe."

"That's the plan," Adam said.

The sheriff nodded. "There are games and books on a shelf in the loft. Help yourselves. Lock up behind me."

He did as she requested then turned to Tara. "Now what?"

"Now I set boundaries." She stuffed her hands into her coat pockets. "There will be no hanky-panky between us while we're here." Her face pinked.

He raised his hands palms out. "You have my word." He was here as a friend, granted one he was very attracted to, but he wouldn't cross any lines.

She nodded. "Good. Thank you."

He grinned.

"What?"

"You're an interesting woman. I'm enjoying getting to know you. Want to play a game to take your mind off things?"

"Not tonight. I'm going to sleep. Or at least try." She grabbed her bag and slung it over her neck and shoulder so it hung down her back then climbed the ladder. "This reminds me of summer camp. I haven't slept in a bunk bed in…forever."

"Same." He was glad she could sleep, but there was no way he would. The sheriff had been careful to make sure they weren't followed, but Tara was his responsibility now, and he aimed to make sure she stayed safe.

Chapter Thirteen

Monday afternoon Nancy sat beside Carter on his living room couch and held his hand. "I haven't had time to work on our wedding."

"I understand. Things have been busy at work for me too. Are you any closer to figuring out who Amelia's mother is?"

"Not really. This thing has blown up in my face." She told him everything that was going on with Tara.

"Wow. So, what's next?"

"For me? Not much. Mom is working on it. I'm not sure we're looking for a local woman."

He rubbed his chin. "How are you handling all of this?"

"Okay, I guess. I had a couple of volunteers at the library, so it went smoothly."

"I'm glad you have them."

"Me too. The way this town keeps growing, I'm going to need to ask for more funding so we can hire additional help." She sighed.

"That was a big sigh. What's wrong?"

"I feel like a failure. This is my first flop as a sleuth, and it smarts."

"You haven't failed yet."

She twisted to face him. "What are you talking about?"

"I might know someone who knows someone who knows someone."

She shook her head. "No way. The more people who get involved in this, the more danger Tara's in. And don't forget my tires were slashed. What if it was a warning to back off?"

"Hasn't stopped you in the past. What's different this time?"

"I've never dealt with a crime syndicate. The word alone freaks me out. They wouldn't hesitate to kill." She shuddered. "I don't want to do anything that would put Tara in more danger."

"Okay, but what if this isn't related? What if it's all a big coincidence?"

She gasped. "You think it is?" If that was the case, she could keep digging without endangering Tara.

"I don't know. I'll talk to your mom tomorrow and see what she's come up with. I suspect she's been working on this all day. Her office door and blinds were closed the entire time I was there."

"Seriously?" That wasn't like Mom. Usually she worked with her deputies, but maybe this was too sensitive. "What I need is a powerwalk with Anna. I think better when walking."

"Why not go and visit her? She must be home by now."

"Good idea." She kissed him then stood. "You're a genius." For the first time since Tara had gone into hiding, she didn't feel helpless. "Love you. I know we talked about a Christmas Eve wedding, but I've been so distracted I haven't follow up on it yet. I'll call the church this week and see about reserving it. Then we won't need to worry about decorating."

He chuckled. "Sounds good. But I think we could

swing a few decorations."

"No need. The church does a wonderful job. How do you feel about forest green and purple for our wedding colors?" She hadn't given that any thought before blurting it, but she seriously didn't care about that kind of stuff.

"If that's what you want."

"I think it is."

He stood and walked her out to her car. "Want me to find a photographer or the baker for our cake?"

"I'll get Pepper to make the cake."

"She's a baker too?"

"Her cakes are amazing. Everything she serves in her shop is her own creation. I only need to tell her the flavor we want."

"Can we have more than one?"

She grinned and wrapped her arms around his neck as they stood beside her car. "I'm sure that can be arranged. Do you have a favorite flavor? I can ask for a sample for you to try."

"Yum. Strawberry for sure. Maybe she will give you several flavors so we can taste test them."

"Mmm. Sounds like a delicious idea. I'll talk to her."

His eyelids closed as his lips met hers. Nancy melted in his arms and murmured against his mouth. "You're making leaving difficult."

He grinned and kissed her again before releasing her. "I love you. Christmas can't get here soon enough."

She giggled and got behind the wheel of her car. She wasn't a giggler, which made her giggle more.

A short while later, she pulled into her driveway

and headed next door to Anna's house, noting no vehicles in front of the house. Good. That meant Anna's boyfriend wasn't there, and she wouldn't be intruding. She rang the doorbell. Freddy barked wildly from the other side of the door. It swung open, and Freddy jumped up at her. "Down boy." She squatted and scratched his back. "Looks like someone needs a walk. Do you have time?" She glanced up at Anna.

"I'd love to walk. Give me five minutes to change, and I'll meet you out front."

"Prefect." Nancy jogged home and quickly changed into her walking clothes and shoes. She found Anna and Freddy waiting on her front porch. "You're fast."

"I can be when I put my mind to it." They set off down the block. Anna gave her a few sideways glances. "What's going on? You don't seem quite yourself." A cat crossed their path, and Freddy's lunged forward. She pulled back on his leash.

"I'm not. Do you remember the baby that was abandoned at the library?"

"Of course. I take it you haven't found her mother?"

"No. And I'm afraid the mom could be in danger." She explained as much as she could without putting Tara and her situation in the middle of it. "So you see, it's now more urgent than ever that I discover who the mom is, not only to make sure she's okay, but to help bring justice."

"You're wrong about one thing."

"What's that?"

"It's not your job to bring justice. As you

requested, I did some digging at work and learned about two pregnant girls. One is still attending classes, and the other dropped out. I heard that the one who left school had her baby recently."

Excitement bubbled through Nancy. "You're kidding? This is great news. Do you think she'd be willing to talk with me?"

Anna frowned. "You know I can't tell you who she is."

Nancy's pace slowed. "Right. I forgot. But I *need* to talk to her."

"I already did. She's living with her parents, and I saw the baby."

"Oh. Then why did you mention her?"

"So you'd know I did as you asked."

"Okay. I understand. But where does that leave me?"

"Well...I'm not naïve enough to believe there aren't other girls that could have been pregnant and simply didn't show enough for anyone to notice. I'll do some more asking around and see what I can find out."

"Have you talked with Maddie?"

"Luke's daughter? I don't know if he would appreciate me asking his daughter a question like that."

Luke and Anna had been seeing one another since last spring. His daughter and Carter's nephew were best friends. "Then I'll ask. She's over at Carter's place often enough. I'll make a point of being there the next time she is."

"Good idea. Things with Luke are too new. Plus, remember how he reacted the last time we tried to get

Maddie to help us.”

“Who could forget?” Carter and Luke had both been very protective, but in the end they’d come around and allowed the teens to help. “But she wouldn’t be in any danger.”

“You sure about that? Seems to me someone in this town is up to no good.” Anna slowed. “I’m worried about you, Nancy. I think this time you need to let the authorities handle it.”

“Maybe, but you know that’s not how I’m wired.” The authorities were doing the best they could, but if there was anything she could do to help, she wanted to do it, not only for Tara’s sake, but for the woman who’d felt compelled to abandon her baby. There had to be a good reason, and that baby deserved to one day know the truth if she wanted to.

“I know. What can I do?”

“You’re doing it. Walking and talking is the best way to help me. It’s during these walks that I think the best.”

“Well, I can certainly do that.”

Gratitude filled Nancy. She might not know which direction to turn at the moment, but she had a small army of people willing to help in any way they could. Even Pepper, though under duress, had been a huge help. Yes, she was blessed. *Lord, thank You for sending me lots of helpers. Now if You’d set me in the right direction, I’d sure appreciate it. I feel like time is running out.*

Day three of being holed up in the cabin, and Tara

was ready to climb the walls. Adam had done his best to entertain her, but there were only so many times they could play checkers or Uno. She whirled around to where Adam sat on the couch, his laptop on his legs and his fingers clicking away on the keys. "I need to get some fresh air."

"Open the window." His focus remained on the computer.

She stuck out her tongue, turned back to the window, and yanked it open. She breathed in deeply of the fir needle scented cool mountain air. Sunshine filled the clear blue sky, making it even harder to stay indoors. "Come on, Adam. You know you want to get out of here."

"Sheriff Daley said to stay put."

"I know, but what's it going to hurt to step outside for a bit."

He stopped typing and looked her way. "This is really hard for you isn't it?"

She nodded. "I get antsy from being indoors."

He grinned. "That's why you walk around the block during your break at work?"

"One of the reasons. I like the exercise too. My body hurts from this inactivity."

He stood and walked over to the window, rocking back on his heels he peered out. "It looks quiet out there."

She held her breath. Would he give in? She could go without him, but the idea of being alone shot uncontrollable fear through her.

"What if the sheriff comes back while we are out?"

She let out her breath. "We won't go far."

He rubbed the back of his neck then looked

outside again before closing and locking the window. "Get your coat. It's brisk even though the sun is shining."

Joy burst through her. Without thinking she jumped in the air. "Yes! Thank you."

He laughed. "Let me guess, you were once a cheerleader."

"Nope. But sometimes the kid in me comes out." Her face heated.

"I like the kid in you." His eyes danced with merriment. He shrugged into his jacket and pulled a slate-colored beanie onto his head.

Tara quickly slipped on Nancy's borrowed coat and pulled up the hood. "Ready."

He grinned and held his hand out to her. "Stay close. I don't want anything to happen to you."

She slipped her cold hand into his warm one. A tingle shot through her fingers. That was a mistake. She liked Adam so much, but they could never pursue their attraction to one another. They'd had fun playing games over the weekend, and talking until the wee hours of the morning, until one of them fell asleep.

There was certainly nothing romantic about the cabin—it was definitely set up for hunters, but she couldn't stop this attraction to him that grew every time they talked. At least Adam slept on a bunk on the far side of the loft from her. It would have felt too intimate having him any closer. Going there simply wasn't an option. Her life was a mess, and she refused to drag him down the path she was on just so she could have him in her life.

Adam squeezed her hand as they left the cabin

behind and ventured into the sunshine. He breathed in deeply. "This is nice. I can see why the sheriff hung onto this place. The location alone is worth whatever it cost her to keep it."

"Mmm-hmm." Birds chirped from nearby fir trees. "Do you think there's a lake nearby?"

"Maybe, but we aren't going to explore to find out."

She frowned even though she knew his caution was for the best.

"Some day I want to go to the Caribbean and take hundreds of pictures." Adam looked wistfully at the blue sky.

"Is that a bucket list item?" she asked.

"I suppose it is. But I hadn't put it in those terms. My dream is to one day save up enough money so I can take a leave of absence from my job to spend several months there writing and exploring. I'd love to write a travel book." His eye lit with excitement as he spoke.

"You should."

"I'd rent a hut on the beach and write for hours uninterrupted." His gaze shifted to her. "What about you? What are your dreams?"

She shrugged. "To be free."

Something snapped to their right. Fear shot through Tara. "We should go back inside," she whispered. It was probably only an animal, but what if it was a two legged one?

Adam's heart nearly pounded out of his chest as they

rushed back to the cabin. At least they hadn't ventured more that a hundred feet or so. He knew better than to venture outside. The sheriff had warned him privately when she'd walked him to his car that whoever was after Tara could be watching them and that taking her to the cabin was not a guarantee of safety. She'd even gone so far as to advise he take along a gun if he owned one. As it happened, he had a conceal and carry license and kept his handgun locked in his glove box. Though the sheriff had arranged to have his SUV removed from the state park and returned to his house, he'd taken the gun with him.

Thankfully the only time he'd ever had need to use it was at the shooting range. He'd taken the safety course required in the state of Oregon for a conceal and carry license and tried to get to the range at least once a month. To his way of thinking, if he was going to carry, he needed to know how to use it safely and with accuracy.

Right out of college he'd dreamed of being an investigative reporter and envisioned himself on a stakeout in the seedy part of some city. He'd gotten the weapon in case of an emergency. His career had gone a different direction, and if the pounding in his chest was an indicator, he'd made the right decision to stay in Tipton and write human-interest stories as well as the occasional crime piece.

He closed the blinds on all the windows.

"What are you doing?"

"If that wasn't an animal but someone up to no good, I don't want them to get a clear shot of either of us."

Her face paled.

His heart melted. "I'm sorry. I didn't mean to frighten you more than you already are."

"No. It's fine. I needed to hear that. It was a bad idea to go outside. I knew better, and I pushed you to go against your better judgment. I'm sorry."

He walked over to her and held out his arms.

She shook her head and stepped back. "I'm going to take a nap."

He dropped his arms to his sides and watched her dart up the ladder faster than he imagined possible. Now she was running from him too? What had he done to scare her?

He frowned as he turned to peer through the slats in the blinds. Everything outside appeared to be normal, but he would email the sheriff and let her know what was going on. Maybe she'd even have good news. He'd offered to come here on impulse, not thinking through how long they could be stuck here. If this went on much longer, Tara wouldn't be the only one going stir crazy.

Chapter Fourteen

TARA HUGGED THE SPARE BED PILLOW as she lay on the bottom bunk bed. She'd made a fool of herself with Adam. All he'd wanted to do was comfort her, and she'd rejected him and probably hurt his feelings in the process. She'd been as frightened as a mouse trapped in a corner with a cat ready to pounce, but she didn't need to fear Adam. He was one of the good guys. After all, he'd dropped everything to keep her company while she was in hiding.

If only she'd listened to her gut and left town when she'd had the chance. But Nancy had been right. She would always be running and looking over her shoulder for the rest of her life unless that crime syndicate was brought to justice. Then again, even if it was, they'd probably put a hit out on her to get even.

She was in a lose-lose situation. No matter what she did, there was no good choice. She wiped away a tear. This was so unfair. She closed her eyes and tried to calm herself by breathing slowly and deeply. *God, I know we haven't been close for a long time, but I'm in over my head. I need You. This situation is scary, and I don't know what to do. Did I make a mistake coming here? What should I do?*

Trust.

Who was she supposed to trust? She punched the pillow and rolled over so she faced the wall, closing out everything around her to allow sleep to take over.

The scent of spicy meat awakened Tara. She stretched then rubbed her eyes and rolled off the bunk. She headed for the ladder and climbed down.

Adam stood at the stove. He looked in her direction. "Hey, sleepyhead."

"Hi. What're you making?"

"Tacos."

"For lunch?"

"Why not? We can have the leftovers for dinner."

She sat at the peninsula. "Do you need any help?"

"Nope."

He turned back to the stove. Awkwardness settled between them. She should address what happened earlier, but would it make things even more difficult than they already were? Who knew how long they'd be stuck up here? She cleared her throat. "I need to apologize for earlier."

"It's fine."

"No. It's not. I acted like an impetuous child demanding to go outside. Then I was rude when you tried to comfort me. I'm sorry. I'm not used to people caring."

He looked over his shoulder. "You're kidding? I've known you exactly a week, and in that time I've seen at least three people go out of their way for you. Nancy took you in when you needed a safe place to stay, her mom didn't have to put you up here and get involved in your situation. She has a lot of stuff to deal with without cleaning up something you started a long time ago. And don't forget Pepper."

"She did that for Nancy."

He shook his head. "You really don't get it, do you? People care about you. You'd know that if you'd give them half a chance."

"How am I supposed to do that when I don't trust my own judgment? I don't have the best track record when it comes to relationship choices."

"So that's why you backed away." It wasn't a question. He turned off the stove and moved the skillet from the burner. "Lunch is ready."

"Can you blame me?"

A storm of emotions crossed his face, ending with resolve. "I get doubting your judgment. I've doubted mine more times than I care to admit. You're a smart woman who fell for the wrong guy. It happens every day to smart women. And yes, men too. Including me. So get over yourself."

Tara closed her gaping jaw. Somewhere deep inside, laughter bubbled and overcame her. She laughed so hard she cried—she'd needed that.

Adam's brow furrowed as he stared at her in disbelief.

She caught her breath, holding a hand to her chest. "I'm sorry for laughing. Maybe the stress is getting to me, but you made me realize that I wasn't being fair to you or even myself. I expect perfection, and when I fail I beat myself up. Thank you for reminding me that no one is perfect. And for the record, I'll get over myself. Thanks for calling me out."

A sheepish look settled on his face. "You're welcome?"

She chuckled. "I'm serious. I wouldn't normally appreciate being spoken to so bluntly, but in this case, I needed it. I don't know how you've managed to understand me so quickly, but you seem to get me."

He rubbed the back of his neck. "And here I thought you were going to kick me out on my rear for talking like that to you."

"Just don't let it happen again." She shot him a grin, so he knew she was teasing. "I'm starving."

"There's plenty."

Adam surreptitiously watched Tara dig into her taco. They'd had their first fight and survived. That had to be a good sign. It still irked him that she thought so little of him, but in a way he understood. Self-doubt was a powerful obstacle that tripped up even the most successful people.

While she'd slept, he'd heard back from the sheriff via an encrypted email. She'd contacted the DEA in Miami. At first she'd hit a wall, but apparently she'd finally said the right thing to the right person— but what she learned only complicated things. She couldn't say when they'd be able to return to civilization but promised to replenish their supplies on Friday night if they were still here. He prayed they wouldn't be but wasn't holding his breath.

Things could move like lightening, or they could go as slow as a sloth. Either way, he'd be here as promised with Tara. He would have done it for anyone but he was especially glad he was stuck here with her. Sure she could be a pain and a little insulting, but he understood the fear behind it and wouldn't hold it against her—at least for long. He snickered.

She stopped mid-bite and glanced at him, raising

a brow.

"Sorry. My mind is wandering."

She bit into the taco, seeming to let it drop. "We need to come up with a schedule."

"For what?"

"Exercising. I can't stand sitting around here all day, and going outside is clearly a bad idea."

"What do you propose? The space here is rather limited." A huge understatement, considering the main floor was probably only three hundred square feet and the loft was half that size.

"Calisthenics. I can do them in place. I'll use cans from the kitchen as weights, and I can run in place to get my heart rate up."

The idea of getting her heart rate up took his mind someplace it shouldn't, and he choked on the food in his mouth. He coughed and gulped some water.

"You okay?"

"Yep. Sorry about that. You were saying?"

"Right." She went on to explain her idea, which was a good one.

"Fine. I can live with that." Too bad he didn't have gym clothes in his emergency bag.

"Thanks for making our meal for today. I'll take care of tomorrow."

He'd tasted what she passed off as food over the weekend. "How about I give you a cooking lesson instead and we make the meal together? I'll teach you how to make one of the meals I learned when I took a class."

She frowned. "My cooking was that bad?"

"I didn't say that. You mentioned the desire to

take a class. I'm here, and we have excess time so why not?"

She shrugged. "Sure. But today, I'm going to find another book to read. If we're here much longer, I'll have read the entire collection on the shelf upstairs."

"Too bad neither of us thought to pick up a few along the way."

"It's fine. Though I never would have chosen to read any of the ones here, it's been interesting reading."

He chuckled. "The book selection is rather eclectic." He'd noticed a couple of international thrillers, romances, fantasy, and a few science fiction novels. Probably left behind by passers-through. "Do you have a favorite?"

"Not really. Although I'm avoiding the thrillers."

"Makes sense." He enjoyed thrillers too much though to not read them simply because of their current circumstances. The sheriff had seemed confident that things would settle soon, so he had to believe the authorities had everything in hand. At least he prayed they did, because even though he had a weapon for protection he didn't want to use it. But he would to keep Tara safe.

Chapter Fifteen

Tuesday morning, Nancy stood in the library and breathed in of the scent of books mingled with the odor of cleaning products. She'd arrived early today to give everything a once-over since she'd neglected to do her normal light cleaning yesterday.

The library doors slid open, and Lacy, her newest volunteer, walked in right on time, wearing leggings and a tunic top along with cute boots. She'd taken Nancy's request that the volunteers dress in business casual to heart.

Nancy smiled. "Good morning, Lacy."

"Hi." Lacy's gaze shifted from side to side.

"Is everything okay?"

Lacy laced her fingers together in front of her. "I'm a little nervous. I don't want to mess up."

"There's nothing to be anxious about. All I need for you to do is return books to the shelves. It's really quite simple." Nancy walked to the cart containing books that needed to be re-shelved and picked one up. She pointed to the spine and explained the code. "Does that make sense?"

"That sounds easy enough."

"Good." Nancy returned the book to the cart. "Follow me, and I'll show you the layout." In under five minutes they were back where they started. "Any questions?"

"Nope. I think I have it."

"Good. If you're unsure about anything, ask. We generally don't get super busy until the afternoon, so I should be able to answer questions as long as I'm not helping someone." She pushed the cart toward Lacy. "Have fun."

Lacy shot a wobbly smile in her direction before heading to the stacks with the cart.

The library had been fortunate this fall to acquire three new volunteers. The timing couldn't have been more perfect since Tara couldn't be here. Nancy's thoughts had drifted to Tara more than once over the weekend. How was she handling being isolated with only Adam to keep her company? At least they got along. It would've been a nightmare for her if they didn't. Then again, Adam wouldn't have volunteered if they got on one another's nerves.

She sat at her computer and attempted to focus on work. She was no closer to finding Amelia's mom than she had been a few days ago. Carter had been hopeful and offered to help, but the sheriff's department had way too much going on between the normal day-to-day stuff and investigating Rachel's death. No one had said as much, but she suspected foul play was involved. Why else would her mom keep the details so quiet?

Normally she'd push them for answers like Adam had been doing, but Rachel's death wasn't relative to her case, so she couldn't afford to divide her time. Speaking of time, she really needed to get busy.

An hour later, Lacy pushed the empty cart back to the checkout counter. "All finished. I can only stay for an hour today, but I'll try to work it out so I can help out longer next time. This was actually fun."

"I'm glad you enjoyed yourself." Although she couldn't imagine how shelving books could be considered fun.

"I discovered several books I want to read once I'm done with my classes."

Now Nancy understood. "Good for you. When will you be back?"

"I'm on the schedule for Friday afternoon."

Nancy had made the schedule, but wanted to make sure Lacy had read it without coming right out and asking. "See you then. Have a great week." She'd hoped Lacy would stick around longer than the hour she'd committed to, but understood being busy and having to leave on time. As it turned out Lacy only needed twenty hours of community service for her class—she'd have it done in no time if she stuck to the schedule Nancy made.

At closing time, Anna strolled into the library. Nancy stood to greet her friend. "This is a surprise."

"I thought you and Tara brainstormed at this time."

"You're right, but not today." She'd kept Anna in the dark about what was going on with Tara and completely forgot they had planned to toss around ideas about who baby Amelia's mom could be. "However, that won't keep us from tossing around ideas. Let me lock up. You want to hang out here or walk?"

Anna rolled her eyes playfully. "Duh. Walk, of course."

Nancy chuckled. "Then let's get out of here."

A half hour later, Anna walked Freddy, her American Eskimo Spitz, on his leash. Nancy pumped her arms willing the gears in her mind to kick in. It had been a challenging day without Tara, and brain fatigue had set in. "Have you learned about any other teen pregnancies?"

"Thankfully no. What about birth records? Did Carter come through with those?" Anna asked.

"No. He's having some trouble with that. The hospital wants a warrant, and the judge won't give him one. I'll have to check the birth announcements in the paper." She should have done that days ago.

"I don't think it will do you any good." Anna kicked through a small pile of leaves.

"Why not?"

"If the woman had planned to give up her baby why would she make a public announcement?"

"You're right." She should have thought of that. "Wishful thinking, I guess. But are we sure she intended to give up Amelia? After all, she named her and cared for her for at least a week." But the drugs in the carrier made her wonder. Nothing added up. Why would a young mother go to the trouble of naming and caring for a baby she planned to abandon, and why did said baby have drugs in her carrier?

"True. She could have been undecided I guess," Anna said. "Or maybe she had planned to keep Amelia but motherhood became too much for her."

"Under those circumstances, she very well may have put an announcement in the paper."

"It's worth looking," Anna said.

"I'll check the paper online when I get back."

They completed the loop around their neighborhood in contemplative silence. At Anna's driveway they parted. Nancy went into her house and straight to her laptop. If there was a clue, she'd find it. She powered on her computer then poured a glass of water while it booted up.

The doorbell rang then the door opened. Nancy ducked behind a wall. Her heart pounded.

"Nancy, it's Mom. Did you know you left your door unlocked?"

"No." She stepped out from behind the wall holding a hand to her chest. "You nearly took ten years off my life."

Mom chuckled. "Sorry. We need to talk."

Adam read the secure email from the sheriff for the third time. This couldn't be right.

Tara climbed down the ladder and looked at him, frowning. "What's wrong?"

He closed the lid to his laptop. "Nothing."

"We might have only met a little over a week ago, but we've been together 24/7 for the past four days, and I can see clearly that something is bothering you. Tell me or not, it's up to you, but they say talking helps."

He held in a chuckle. "You know this from personal experience? Because from where I sit you're mighty closed off. I imagine you haven't had a heart-to-heart with anyone in years."

She crossed her arms and raised her chin. "So what if I haven't? It's not like there's been anyone to confide in, much less anything I can say."

"Seriously?" He patted the space beside him on

the couch.

She hesitated then sat as far into the corner of the couch as possible.

He took a breath and let it out. "I understand why you've kept to yourself, but I know your secret and you still haven't opened up about anything."

She avoided eye contact. "It never crossed my mind."

"I would think not, considering how hard you've worked at protecting those in your life. But you don't need to protect me. I've watched you wander around this cabin, or hide out up in the loft for days. You hardly speak. I, for one, need a little noise and human contact."

She frowned. "I guess I've grown accustomed to silence."

He imagined so, considering she spent her work hours in a quiet library and had no social life. "But you *do* remember what it was like to have people who care about you in your life. People who want to hear about your day—your fears, your joy, anything at all."

She nodded and took an unsteady breath. Her gaze met his. Her eyes filled with anguish.

"Ah, Tara. I didn't mean to upset you."

She shrugged. "It's fine. I'm not upset."

"Liar."

She looked away. After a moment, she spoke softly. "I met Patrick at work. He was charming, smart, helpful, and he knew how to treat a lady. He was perfect." She frowned. "Or, so I thought. We'd dated about a year when I started to notice little things."

"Such as?" Adam asked.

"He was busy all the time. We used to spend a lot of time together outside of work then gradually our time together became less frequent to the point I thought he was seeing someone else."

"So you followed him." It made sense. He'd have thought the same.

"Yes, and that's when everything changed." Her tortured eyes met his. "Life as I knew it ceased to exist."

"You started over in Tipton, but you've only been existing outside the walls of the library."

"You know me better than I realized. How?" She rolled her eyes. "Never mind. I know."

"You do?" he asked.

"Absolutely. You're a keen observer. It's part of being a journalist. You notice things others miss, like the seemingly mundane and unimportant things."

His face heated. "Seems to me you're good at observing as well." Either she'd been paying attention, or she had a gift for understanding human nature—maybe a little of both.

"I had to learn. My life depended on it."

He nodded. "You mentioned you employed a private investigator."

"Yes. He keeps an eye on my family and reports to me once a week."

"When did you last hear from him?"

"He calls me every Wednesday. But Nancy has my phone." Panic filled her voice. "I have to answer that call. If I don't, he'll think the worst has happened. We made a plan that if a week goes by that he's unable to reach me he should assume I'm dead and stop watching my family since they'd no longer be in danger if I'm dead."

Adam sucked in a breath. "Whose cockamamie idea was that? There are a number of reasons why a person would be unavailable."

"I suppose, but it's never been an issue."

"Does he know where you live?"

"Yes."

"I'll contact Nancy and let her know about the call. It's going to be okay." He reached out and grasped her hand. "There's something you should know though."

Fear filled her eyes. "What?"

"I've been in contact with the sheriff. The DEA is aware of this group that you told us about, and they have someone deep undercover with them, but they aren't yet ready to take them down."

"Why not?"

"I don't know."

"Where does that leave me?"

"Sheriff Daley is coming on Friday. We can ask her then."

She pulled her hand free and stood. "That's three days away!" She paced to the front window with her hands propped at her waist. "I have responsibilities, and so do you."

"I know." He kept his voice calm and stood.

She held up a hand palm out. "Stop. It's hard enough to deal with all of this without complicating our relationship."

"What are you talking about?" All he did was stand, since it felt rude to sit when she wasn't.

She waved a hand between them. "This. Us. I'm attracted to you, and unless I'm a complete moron, you share similar feelings. But right now, I can't deal with that. I need to focus on staying alive."

She certainly knew how to be blunt. "Fair enough. I respect that." He held out his hand to her. "Friends?" It wasn't what he wanted, but if that's all she'd take then he would accept it—for now.

She hesitated then grasped his hand and shook it firmly before stuffing her fingers into her pants pocket. "Now what?"

"I email Nancy."

Chapter Sixteen

Wednesday morning, Nancy worked quickly to check-in books before opening time. Midweek had become one of the libraries busiest days, and she probably wouldn't have time to deal with anything except the people who needed her help.

Her mom had dropped a bomb last night when she announced there was nothing she could do for Tara other than help her get into witness protection, assuming she was willing to testify to what she saw that night. The problem was, Nancy didn't think Tara would go for that.

But the other thing her mom said still had her reeling—the DEA stated that the drugs found with baby Amelia were not connected to the crime syndicate in Florida, which meant they had no clue who was behind the drugs. If they were unrelated to what was going on, did that mean Tara's location was unknown and she was still safe?

Nancy checked in the final book, then quickly pushed the cart of books to the stacks. She had twenty minutes before the library opened—no problem, but she could hardly wait for Tara to come back. She not only missed the woman's help but her company as well. Sure the volunteers were great, and she enjoyed visiting with the library patrons, but Tara had become a fixture in her life—even if they weren't close.

She had to figure this out. She'd lain in bed awake for half the night pondering everything that had happened in Tipton over the past week and a half. Was any of it connected? Was all of it connected? Or were they simply random acts? Unfortunately she was no closer to an answer this morning than she was last night.

The alarm on her phone beeped—time to open the library. She pushed the cart over to her desk and left it there, then unlocked the doors. Lacy breezed in.

"Good morning," Nancy said. "This is a surprise."

"A pleasant one I hope. My classes this morning were cancelled, so I thought, why not get in a couple of volunteer hours. Do you mind?"

"Not at all, I only wish I'd known. I came in early today to get the books checked in and shelved." She yawned. She wouldn't have gotten up so early.

"I didn't know sooner. I'm sorry." Lacy's gaze roved the library. "Is there something else you need done? Dusting or..." she shrugged, "whatever."

She didn't have time right now to train Lacy to do anything. But those crime stats still needed to be entered into the computer. "How are you at typing?"

Her face brightened. "Fast."

"Perfect. Let's get you set up on the computer."

Five minutes later Nancy took the lid off the box containing the oldest records for Tipton county. "Anything sensitive has been redacted. All you need to do is fill in the template with the correct information." At least when she'd started this project way back when, she'd created a template, making it only a matter of data input.

"Sounds easy."

"Thanks. You're welcome to stop in anytime to do this. Data entry is not my favorite task."

"No problem. Maybe I'll be able to complete the entire project."

"That would be incredible if you could. I imagine your remaining nineteen hours might be enough. I'll let you get to it."

The library doors slid open again, and the normal crowd of homeschoolers entered. "Good morning!" She enjoyed this group. Some had a little more energy than she appreciated in the library, but overall, they were respectful and seemed to have a sincere love for books.

At some point during the morning rush, Lacy must have slipped out because she'd abandoned the boxes, and Nancy didn't see her anywhere. Curious about how much she'd accomplished, Nancy wiggled the mouse to wake up the computer. She scrolled through the template. "Not bad." It looked like she'd entered four years' worth of crime stats. At this rate Lacy would for sure finish the project.

Nancy's stomach growled. She looked longingly toward the exit. As much as she enjoyed the library, she could use some fresh air and conversation with a friend. If only someone else could take over for an hour. Resigned to her situation, she plopped onto her desk chair and pulled out a sandwich. Maybe she could get it eaten before anyone wandered in.

The library doors slid open. Nancy grinned. "Hey, Carter." She stood, setting her sandwich aside.

He strolled over to her. "How's it going?"

"Fine. I'm feeling sorry for myself for being stuck here, but seeing you makes up for it."

He brushed his lips across hers. "I'm glad. I might have a lead for you."

"Really?" Excitement bubbled inside her. "What?"

He kept his voice low. "I was finally able to access the birth records for the two weeks prior to Amelia showing up here."

"And?" Had he found something significant?

"I emailed them to you a few minutes ago."

"Yes!"

He chuckled.

She glanced up at him. "What?"

"I enjoy watching you work a puzzle. Let me know if anyone stands out to you. I need to get back to work."

Her insides deflated. "So soon?"

"Yes, sorry. Did you remember to call the church about booking the wedding?"

She snapped her fingers. "Sweet junipers. I'll do right now."

He raised a brow. "What about the birth records?"

"They aren't going anywhere." She shot him a saucy grin and reached for the phone. A few minutes later she hung up. "Someone already booked the sanctuary for Christmas Eve. I didn't think anyone would want the sanctuary after the service. Now what do we do?" She stared at her computer screen and spotted an email from Adam—that was odd. She clicked on the email and frowned.

"What is it?" Carter asked.

"Tara's PI guy calls her every Wednesday. Apparently if she doesn't answer, that's supposed to mean she's dead. She wants me to make sure I take his call."

"You're kidding? Do you have her phone?"

"No." She winced. "It's on my dresser." Her gaze met Carter's. "What do I do? I can't leave."

"I'll go. Give me the keys."

She pulled keys from her purse and dropped them in the palm of Carter's hand. "What if he's already called?"

"Don't borrow trouble. I'll be back as soon as I can." He turned and hustled out the door. Nancy stood, unable to sit still, and walked around the library. A young woman sat at a desk off in a corner. Nancy stopped short—she thought the library was empty. They'd kept their conversation low, but had the woman heard? She cleared her throat "Hi. Angie. I didn't see you come in."

Angie looked up from the book she was reading. "I arrived when all those kids were here and decided to find a quiet corner to read."

Nancy grinned. "Must be a good book because I don't think any quiet corners exist when that many kids are set free in the library at once."

Angie giggled. "I think you're right. Do you have any kids of your own?"

"No. How about you?"

A shadow blipped across her face then disappeared. Nancy would have missed it if she'd blinked. "No kids. Maybe someday, but I'm not ready for that kind of responsibility right now."

"What do you do with your time?"

"I blog."

"You can make a living by blogging?"

"With the right advertisers, yes. I post book reviews on one of my blogs, and my other blog is all about young adult life. I touch on all topics related to being a young adult, like college, friends, dating. You get the picture."

"That's seriously cool."

Angie pulled a card from her purse and handed it to Nancy. "Those are my sites."

"I'll check them out. Thanks. Will you excuse me, Angie? I need to find a venue for my wedding while things here are quiet." Now that the church was out, where would they get married?

"No problem. When's the big day."

"Christmas Eve."

Angie laughed. "Any place worth having will be booked by now. What happened?"

"I assumed, incorrectly, that my church would be available."

Angie nodded. "Good luck."

"Thanks. It sounds like I'm going to need it." *Lord, I messed up. Please help me figure this out. I don't want to disappoint Carter.*

She sat at her desk and did a search for wedding venues in Oregon. So many possibilities filled the page—all very expensive, and like Angie said, they were unavailable. She should have called the church the same day Carter proposed. Maybe they should be unconventional and get married in someone's house. Or wait...what about here? Getting married in the library couldn't be more unconventional, but who cared. They couldn't hold the reception here, but Pepper might be able to help with that. It wasn't like the coffee shop would be open on Christmas Eve anyway.

Nancy pulled her cell phone from her pocket. Her

thoughts went to Tara—she sure hoped she hadn't missed that call. She opened her phone app and pressed Pepper's name in her contacts.

"Nancy? Is everything okay? It's not like you to call during the work day."

"I know. I'll make this fast. I messed up big time by procrastinating. The church is already booked on Christmas Eve. We can use the library for the wedding, but we'd need someplace else for the reception."

"You want to do it here?"

"Do you mind?"

"Not at all. I'd do anything for you. I'd love to cater your reception here."

"Really? I was thinking cake, punch, tea, and an open coffee bar."

"Oh. Well that's unique," Pepper said. "I have an idea for your cake. How many guests will you have?"

"I'm cutting us off at one hundred, and I'm hoping for fewer."

"I'll need a fairly firm headcount."

"Guess I should get the invitations ordered. And don't do a huge cake. I'm thinking two tiers and then mini cupcakes."

"Got it. Wait! You haven't ordered your invitations yet?" Pepper's shock reverberated in her voice.

"I've been busy."

"All brides are busy. I love you, Nancy, but you need to get your act together."

Nancy's stomach knotted. "You're right. I'll do better." Maybe she should have hired that wedding coordinator Anna mentioned. It was probably too late now though.

"Good. I'll see you Friday morning?"

"Yes. Thanks for doing this."

"That's what friends are for."

"Oh. I forgot. Will you be one of my bride's maids?"

"I thought you'd never ask. I'd be honored. Who's your maid of honor?"

"I don't have one. You and Anna are my bridesmaids, so I guess you're equally my maids-of-honor too."

"Oh, Nancy," dismay filled Pepper's voice, "you're doing everything wrong."

Nancy's shoulders slumped. "I don't want to choose between my two best friends."

"It's fine. I need to go."

Nancy pocketed her phone with a sigh. She should have asked Carter to plan their wedding. He was the one who cared so much about it. Now guilt nipped at her for not trying harder. The wedding was important to Carter and therefore should have been a priority for her and she had neglected it—no more. He'd entrusted her with planning their wedding, and she'd failed—big time. Hopefully it wasn't too late to salvage it.

Angie headed in her direction. "See you." She waved and left without checking out any books—odd. Angie generally borrowed the limit and returned them on time too. She shrugged off the thought as Carter entered the library for the second time that day.

She rushed toward him. "You have the phone?"

"I do, and the PI called already. I answered. He

wasn't willing to talk to me. Said he'd try later."

"Did you explain to him what was going on?" Nancy asked.

"Not really."

"Why not?"

"He didn't give me a chance." He shrugged. "I can give the phone to your mom and let her know the situation. She can decide how to move forward."

"I suppose that's best." She bit down on her bottom lip. "We need to talk."

A worry line etched Carter's forehead. "What's wrong now?"

She explained about what she'd come up with for their wedding venue and reception, watching his face for any sign he was disappointed.

He grinned wide. "I love it. What better place, besides our church, could we get married? The library is perfect. It'll need decorations. Where you able to book our pastor or was he already busy?"

"I didn't think to ask. I'll call the church back. If he can't do it, I know someone else we could ask."

"Sounds good. Also, I'll meet with a florist if you don't want to."

Oh, she loved this man! She took his hands in hers. "Let's do it together."

He pulled her close. "Sounds like a good plan. How did Pepper take the news that we aren't serving food?"

Nancy shook her head. "It could have been better. Are we making a mistake not serving anything other than dessert and a beverage bar?"

"I don't think so. The ceremony won't get over

until after eight."

"Are you disappointed with how things are turning out? Pepper scolded me."

His face softened. "Not at all." His lips met hers in a toe-tingling kiss.

Someone's throat cleared behind Nancy.

She jumped back and looked toward the sound. "May I help you?" she asked a man she didn't recognize.

"I'm looking for this woman. I was told I might find her here." He held up a picture of Tara with long hair.

Carter stepped closer to the man. "Is she in some kind of trouble?"

"Maybe. She's my sister. My family is worried about her. We heard she might be around here."

"Sorry, we can't help," Carter said. "Do you have a card or something with your number so we can call if we spot her?"

He shook his head. "If you haven't seen her, then I doubt you will. She's apparently been here for a while. Thanks for your time."

Nancy's heart thudded as the man left. "Who was that?"

"I don't know, but I intend to find out. Will you send me a still shot from the security footage?"

"Of course. What are you going to do?"

"Run it through facial recognition. That guy was not her brother any more than you're my sister."

"You picked up on that too, huh? But what if he shows her picture around town and someone recognizes Tara and blabs?"

"I'd say that's already happened, which is why he was here. Will you be okay alone?"

"Of course. Go. I'll pull up the photo right now." She sat at her desk and accessed the footage, then took a screen shot of the man when he looked directly at the camera. He sure wasn't afraid to have his face seen—why not?

Chapter Seventeen

WEDNESDAY EVENING TARA RECLINED ON THE couch with a satisfied tummy. The left-over tacos fixings were even better than they'd been at lunch. Plus it was super easy to reheat the meat and fill the shells—no extra cooking necessary. If she wasn't careful, she'd gain so much weight that her clothes wouldn't fit.

"You want to play a game?" Adam asked from the loft.

"Sure." She'd planned to read, but she'd been doing that most of the day.

"How about dominos?"

"Sounds good to me." She closed her eyes and rested her head on the pillow she'd propped against the arm of the couch. "Do you want to play at the coffee table or at the kitchen peninsula?" The kitchen would be easiest, but she was so comfy, moving didn't appeal.

"Here's fine."

Her eyes flew open as Adam dumped out the box of dominos on the coffee table.

"That was fast. I didn't hear you come down." He had serious stealth skills when it came to moving around. "I need to tie a bell to you, so I can hear you coming."

He laughed. "I'd like to see you try." He winked. "I haven't played this since I was a kid."

"Really? My family and I used to play it all the

time." At the mention of her family sadness washed over her. She refused to wallow in it though. "My dad was the best. I think he won almost every game."

A knock on the door made her jump.

Adam motioned her toward the bathroom. "Lock the door and stay quiet," he said in a low voice.

She didn't have to be told twice. She darted as fast as her feet would move.

"Who is it?" Adam spoke loudly.

Tara couldn't hear the reply.

"Thanks, but I'm good."

A moment later he knocked on the bathroom door. "You can come out."

She flipped the lock and flung open the door. "Who was that?" Her heart still pounded like an out-of-control bronco.

"She said she was with the property management company and wanted to know if we needed anything."

Tara frowned. "Are you concerned? What if the woman isn't who she claimed to be?"

"A little. Which is why I'm sending an email to the sheriff right now." He pulled out his smart phone. His thumbs flew across the tiny keyboard with the skill of a teenager.

"The good news is, the woman left. I watched her drive off before I told you it was safe to come out."

"And the bad news?" Tara's voice wobbled.

The reply pinged.

His face paled. He held out the phone to Tara. "It's from Sheriff Daley."

Called property management. Someone claiming to be me phoned and asked them to check on you. Get out! I'll meet you at a diner a couple miles up the highway. Keep out of site as much as possible. I'll call for backup and meet you there. Might be as long as two hours. Stay safe.

"We need to leave. Now!" Adam said. "If it'll fit in your go-bag bring it, otherwise it stays. Got it?"

Tara didn't reply. She nearly flew up the ladder, grabbed her bag, tossing in a few scattered items then climbed back down.

Adam stood at the door wearing his backpack over a coat. He flipped off the lights when her feet touched the floor. "Stay close."

"Okay. But what if she's waiting for us at the end of the driveway?"

"I'm armed. But I don't think she's the one we need to worry about. Whoever tricked her into coming here is." Adam grasped Tara's trembling hand. "Do you mind if I pray?"

"Please do."

He bowed his head. "Lord, we're in a scary situation. We don't know friend from foe, and we need your help. Please guide our footsteps tonight and protect us from harm. In Jesus name, we ask. Amen."

"Amen," Tara echoed. "Let's go."

He cracked the door and peered out. "I don't see anyone."

Tara's eyes had adjusted to the darkness when he turned off the lights. His must have adjusted as well. Crickets chirped in a cacophony of noise that overpowered any other sounds.

"Stay close."

Tara gripped the hem of his jacket. At least it wasn't raining, and the ground wasn't very muddy. "Do you know the way?"

"We'll follow the roadway but stay as near the brush as possible until we get to the highway. The place we're meeting her is further up the pass. I've seen it before. We'll stick close to the bushes along the side of the road and step out of sight if any cars pass by."

"What if someone spots us anyway?"

"I don't know, Tara."

She pushed aside her fear. God had been with her through everything. He was with them now, and she trusted Him to keep them safe. She released her grip on the hem of Adam's jacket and lengthened her stride to walk beside him. The stars and moon were bright enough to see where her feet fell.

A twig snapped nearby. She stopped cold, her heart slammed into her chest. "What was that?" she whispered.

"I don't know. Keep moving."

She did as he instructed. Her pulse thrummed in her ears. She didn't want to be afraid. She trusted God to take care of her. She needed His peace—the kind that surpassed all understanding or logic.

Headlights lit the roadway. They ducked into the brush until it passed.

"Do you think the diner will be open?"

"No idea." He wrapped his hand around hers once the car passed. "Let's keep going."

Although it felt longer, not more than forty minutes had passed when she spotted a small parking lot ahead. "Is that it?"

"Yes, and it looks open."

"Are you sure we should we go inside?" she asked.

"Yes. That's what the sheriff said to do, so that's what we'll do. Besides, we'd probably draw more attention to ourselves by hanging out in the parking lot than if we went in and ordered dessert."

"Okay."

They walked in, holding hands, and were greeted by a sign that said to seat themselves. Three tables were occupied by couples who didn't give them more than a glance as they walked across the dining area. They found a booth that allowed a good view of the entrance, but kept them out of view of anyone looking in from the outside.

A moment later a blonde woman wearing jeans and a black T-shirt approached them. "Can I get you started with anything to drink?"

"Do you have tea?" Tara asked.

The waitress rattled off several choices.

"Herbal mint please."

"I'll have coffee, please." Adam handed her the menu. "If you have any apple pie left, we'll share a piece." He looked to Tara as if he wanted her approval.

She nodded, even though there was no way she'd be able to eat anything. "How long do you think we'll be able to sit here before she gets annoyed?"

He shrugged. "So long as we leave a generous tip, I don't think she'll mind too much. It's not like this place has a line of people waiting for a table."

It would take Sheriff Daley at least another hour to get to them, assuming she left right away and didn't get slowed down. Sitting here that long shouldn't raise any suspicion—she hoped.

Nancy reached for her ringing phone on her bedside table—the third call she'd had in the last hour. She'd gone to bed early tonight and should have turned off her cell phone. "Hello." She tried to sound pleasant but winced when annoyance was evident in her tone.

"Nancy, it's Mom. I'm out front. I need your help." She explained about Adam's email. While she explained, Nancy quickly dressed, slipped her arms into her warmest coat, and donned her favorite boots. "Does Carter know?"

"Yes. I've filled him in. He wanted to come, but I told him no."

"Why? You need backup." As much as Mom liked to think of herself as a one of the deputies, she was still the sheriff. The deputies were better equipped than the sheriff who was more a figurehead than a cop.

"Lyle is with me. But I want you to come along for Tara. My gut says she's going to need you tonight."

"I'll be right out. "Nancy stuffed her phone, wallet, and keys into her pockets and rushed to the waiting car idling in the driveway. She pulled open the door to the backseat and slid in. The dome light shone brightly enough for her to see the worry lines on her mom's face. She clicked on her seatbelt as they backed out.

Lyle had a tablet open on his lap. "Mary says you're up to speed on Tara's case, but there's something you don't know."

Nancy leaned forward. Since when did Lyle use

her mom's first name? Interesting. "What don't I know?"

"U.S. Marshals are in route to the location where Adam and Tara are waiting. They were closer so they should beat us. If Tara will agree to testify to what she witnessed in Florida she will—"

Nancy refused to listen the rest of his words. She knew what was coming next. Tara would be out of her life forever and everyone else's who cared about her. On top of that, she'd have no hope of reconnecting with her family. What about Adam? They were just getting acquainted and seemed like the perfect match for one another. She swallowed the news like a bitter pill. "Does she know?"

"Not yet," Mom said.

"It's been hard for her to not have contact with her family, but she's always had reports from her private investigator to keep her up-to-date on how they're doing. She won't have that anymore." Nancy's stomach sickened as she spoke her thoughts out loud.

"No," Mom said. "She won't, but this is the best option. Even though the syndicate in Florida is not associated with what is going on in Tipton, she would be wise to take the offer of protection and start fresh."

Nancy agreed, but she didn't like it. Is that what the mom who left her baby at the library was trying to do, have a fresh start? Seemed like a cruel way to go about it, but she had a feeling there was more to the story.

They sped along Highway 22 and on through Salem. "How do the authorities know our case isn't tied to Florida?"

"They have someone in deep cover high up in the organization," Lyle said. "This is a coincidence."

"I don't know. I realize there are drugs everywhere, but the circumstances are suspicious to me," Nancy said.

"Things aren't always as they appear." Her mom shifted in her seat.

"True. Do you really believe none of this is connected?" Nancy simply couldn't accept that.

"I trust the DEA knows what it's doing," her mom said.

Nancy wasn't so sure. Mom was obligated to trust them, but she wasn't. She still felt like there was a connection between Tara's past, the library, and the baby. She'd been wrong before though, and she didn't have anything on which to base this opinion. She took a breath and let it out in a huff.

Lyle twisted to look at Nancy. "What are you thinking?"

"That I'm on the cusp of blowing this wide open, but I've got nothing but my gut to back me up."

He frowned. "Be careful, Nancy. We aren't talking about a petty crime. These kind of people will kill you without thinking twice."

"Why so quiet, Mom?"

"I've been praying. If there was ever a time to pray it's now. We are too far away to be of any help to Tara and Adam if they were found by someone intending to harm Tara."

Until her mom's last words, she hadn't realized exactly how grave a situation Tara and Adam were in. *Lord please be with them and protect them.*

Alert for trouble, Adam barely tasted the apple pie their server had delivered moments ago. He'd had a few stakeouts over the years that raised his blood pressure, but nothing like this. *Lord, I know You are in control. I trust You to take care of us. Please give me peace and guidance. I feel like something big is about to happen. We need You.*

Tara's pale face spoke volumes to her state of mind. He placed his hand on top of the table, palm up. She rested her ice-cold fingers in his palm. "I'm scared."

"I know, but I believe we're going to get out of this."

"How do you know?"

"I have faith in God too, but life doesn't always turn out the way we want and bad things happen. That being said, I don't feel like either one of us is going to meet our Maker today." That was about the only thing he felt certain of.

Tara gasped. "What's *he* doing here?"

He looked at the man in question. "Who is he?"

"Buck. The private investigator I hired to keep an eye on my parents. He's coming our way. What do we do?"

"Stay calm." His heart thudded so hard he was sure Tara could see his shirt moving. "You told me he calls with an update about your family every Wednesday."

"He does. Something must be wrong." She stood and rushed toward him.

Buck grabbed her by the arm and pulled her out the door.

"Tara!" Adam stood and raced after her. A few people stared at him as he ran into the parking lot and looked from left to right—no one. He ran around the side of the building. The man had a gun to Tara's head. Adam pulled the gun from his coat pocket and aimed it at the man's head. "I wouldn't do that if I were you. You shoot her, I'll shoot you."

"Oh, yeah." The P.I. shifted the barrel in the flash of an eye and fired at him.

Tara screamed.

Adam jumped behind a dumpster. The bullet hit the metal, making his ears ring. That hadn't gone like he'd expected—at all. Now what?

Tired squealed. Car doors slammed. He chanced a peek around the dumpster. Two men shielded by a black sedan aimed guns at Tara and the man holding her.

"U.S. Marshals. Put the gun down."

Tara stomped on the man's foot then twisted free. She raced toward the dumpster. A single shot fired. Tara screamed and dove onto the hard pavement.

"Are you hit?"

"No." She sucked in a sharp breath and looked at the palm of her hand.

He waved her toward him. "Get over here then. It looks like the Marshals have things under control." He reached out to her. His heart in his throat, he blinked back a rush of emotion. He'd come to care deeply for this woman over the past few days. If she'd been hit...he couldn't go there. He pulled her into his arms once she was close enough and breathed in deeply the vanilla scent of her hair. He ran his hands up and down her arms. "You're sure you're not hit?"

"I'm okay. My hands and knees hurt, but that's all."

"Thank God." He cradled her face in his hands and kissed her.

She stiffened, then relaxed and kissed him back, taking them to a place he hadn't expected.

"A-hem. Excuse me," one of the marshals said.

They pulled apart. Tara giggled then recovered and cleared her throat. "Thanks for saving my life. How did you know where we were?"

"Sheriff Daley. We happened to be within an hour's drive when we got the call."

Tara leaned into Adam. "Thank you. If you'd been a few minutes later..."

"My partner has your assailant in custody. Backup is on the way. From what I've been told the two of you have had a rather eventful evening."

"You can say that again." Adam pocketed his gun and stood, bringing a shivering Tara with him. "Her coat is inside. May I take her in to get it?"

"We'll all go together," the marshal said.

They walked to the front entrance and went inside. The few people who'd been in there when the P.I. had grabbed Tara rushed them and spoke at once.

"Quiet down. I'm U.S. Marshal Jacobs. Everything is under control. Someone will take all of your statements, so please don't leave."

Tara slid her arms into Nancy's coat that was at least one size too big, but Adam imagined she didn't care about that right now.

About twenty minutes later, Nancy strode into the diner.

Adam waved. "Nancy's here."

Tara's head snapped in that direction. She stood.

Nancy rushed to Tara and pulled her into a quick hug. "Are you okay? I heard what happened. Mom and Lyle are outside talking with one of the marshals."

"Other than a few scratches and having ten years scared off my life, I'm fine." Tara sat back down, and Nancy eased into the seat beside her. "What's going to happen, now? No one will tell me anything. I don't understand why Buck tried to abduct me or why the marshals are here."

Adam followed Nancy's gaze as she looked around the diner. A local deputy spoke with a witness across the room, but otherwise the place had cleared out little by little after witnesses had been interviewed.

She shifted to face Tara. "It appears safe to talk here. This is what I know. In the beginning, your private investigator did as you requested, but it appears that at some point, he joined the payroll of the crime syndicate in Florida that you were running from."

Tara's eyes widened. "How? Why?"

"I don't know the details. What I do know is that when my mom made some inquiries about the syndicate, someone in their ranks found out and sent your P.I. to take care of you."

"But why now, after all this time?"

"Apparently they weren't worried about you so long as you were too scared to talk. Once they learned you talked to Buck—"

Tara put up a hand to stop Nancy. "I get it. He was sent to kill me. What about my family?"

"I'm sorry, I don't know."

Adam's heart broke at the distress on Tara's face. "I'll go ask the authorities about your family."

"Don't leave me." She reached out and grasped his wrist.

His brow rose and his heart warmed at the affection that shined in her eyes. How could they possibly have a future? She would go into witness protection, and he would go back to his life in Tipton. There was no hope for them. If only he could go with her, but was that what he really wanted? He loved his family and didn't want to leave them.

Nancy stood. "I'll go find out what I can. Be back soon." She shot them a knowing look.

"Tara, have you thought about what you're going to do?" Adam asked.

She shook her head. "I don't want to leave y— Tipton. But I also don't want to endanger anyone."

He stroked the top of her hand with his thumb. "What if there was a way to stay and not put anyone in danger?"

"How?" She shook her head. "You're dreaming if you think something like that is possible."

"Well it might not be, but it's worth a shot. Don't you want to see where this is going between us?"

She nodded. "Very much."

"Then I say we do everything possible to try and make that happen." He had an idea, but it was a long shot to say the least.

Chapter Eighteen

NANCY STARED OUT THE LIBRARY WINDOW, unable to focus on her job. Her eyes burned from lack of sleep. She'd had maybe three hours of slumber before her alarm went off this morning. She felt for her mom and Lyle. Their night was probably even longer.

Carter strode into the library in his deputy uniform. "Good morning, gorgeous." He had a hand behind his back.

Her heart skipped. "Hi, handsome. How's it going?"

"It's quiet today." He brought his hand out from behind his back and presented her with a giant coffee cup from Roaster's. "I thought you might need this."

Her eyes widened, and a smile stretched her mouth. "Thank you." She grasped the cup between both hands and breathed in the scent of the rich brew through the hole in the top. "What kind is it?"

"A mocha. I know it's not your regular drink, but I figured you needed chocolate too."

She sipped the sweet drink. Ordinarily she'd have preferred plain coffee, but the sweet drink hit the spot this morning. "Thank you. Have I told you lately how much I love you?"

"Hmm. I don't think so."

"Well, I love you a lot."

"Good. Because I love you too. Speaking of love. I'm meeting with the florist about our wedding after my shift today. You want to join me?"

"Sure."

His face lit then a frown puckered his brow. "Are you going to be okay on your own today?"

"I'll manage." Since Tara had been swept away by the marshals, Nancy needed to hire someone soon, even if it was only temporary. She had no idea when or if her assistant would be returning.

"Okay," Carter said. "I need to go. See you later."

"Sounds good." She clicked on her computer and posted the job opening. The morning passed in a blur.

Around noon Lacy strolled into the library. "Hi, Nancy. I heard that your helper is still out. Is there anything I can do to assist you?"

Ah, the joys of small-town life. Everyone knew everything about each other—except when it came to dark secrets, apparently. "How would you like to learn how to check books in and out?"

"Sounds fun." She shrugged off her backpack purse. "Where can I put this?"

"Under my desk."

Lacy deposited her bag under the desk then pulled a chair beside Nancy. "It's too bad we don't have a self-check computer. I've seen those in Salem, and they make things so much faster."

"They're nice, but not in our budget." Nancy went on to explain the procedure for checking out books and then explained how to check them back into the system.

"That sounds easy enough." Only a hint of nervousness filled Lacy's voice. At least she was more relaxed this time than last.

"Good. I'll grab the books from the bin outside,

and you can process them while I watch. If you don't
have any trouble, I'm going to take a quick break to
grab something for lunch. That is, if you can stick
around."

"I can. What do I do if the phone rings?"

"Let voicemail answer." Nancy retrieved the bin of
returned books then went back to her desk. "Your
teacher sure had great timing with this service
project. The help right now is so appreciated. You
have no idea."

Lacy grinned. "I'm glad." She followed Nancy's
instructions exactly, and after a few books, Nancy felt
comfortable leaving the young woman alone. She shot
off a text to Pepper with her lunch order. "I won't be
gone long—ten or fifteen minutes tops. You going to
be okay on your own?"

"Sure. It's not like this place is busy."

"It ebbs and flows. Can I get you anything while
I'm out?" Nancy grabbed her purse.

"No thanks."

"Okay. I'll hurry." Nancy rushed out. Lacy wasn't
overly familiar with the library so she didn't want to
leave her there alone any longer than necessary. On
the way out she nearly bumped into Angie.

"Oh, is the library closing?" Angie frowned.

"No. There's a volunteer inside. I'm grabbing a
sandwich. I'll be right back."

Angie nodded.

A short while later, Nancy walked up to the
counter at Roaster's Coffee.

Pepper held up a brown sack. "I added a dozen
mini cupcakes for you and Carter to taste. I'd like to
narrow down your flavor choices for the reception.

There are six to choose from. Pick three.”

“Okay. Thanks.” She handed over a twenty-dollar bill. “I’m seeing Carter tonight. I’ll let you know tomorrow when we meet for coffee and donuts.”

“Perfect.” Pepper gave her the change. “See you then.” Her attention turned to her next customer. This was why they always got together early on Friday mornings. Even though it was a coffee shop, she had a steady lunch crowd.

Nancy waved to a couple of people in passing, and few minutes later, walked into the library. Warm air whooshed over her as she entered. Lacy stood at the copy machine beside an elderly man. It looked like Lacy was a natural at customer service. Good. Maybe Nancy would be able to eat her sandwich before her helper had to leave.

She studied the young woman, and for the first time wondered what she did to support herself. She’d heard of people depending on student loans for that, but to her way of thinking that was a very costly idea.

Nancy grabbed her sandwich from the bag then deposited her sack with the cupcakes in the book mending room where they kept a mini fridge. She turned to go but startled when Lacy stood in the doorway. “What’s up?”

“A woman would like to speak with you.”

“Okay, thanks. I’m coming.” *So much for eating lunch.* Nancy dropped the sandwich back into the bag then went out to her desk where Angie stood.

“You’re still here.”

“Yes. I was talking to Lacy about volunteering. She said to talk to you.”

“That’s great. I’ll take all the help I can get, but I

thought you had a full-time job with your blog and all the reading you do."

"That's true, but I want to give back too. Ever since the day Krista and I came in and you were taking care of that baby, I've been thinking how fun it would be to help out here. I'd never noticed anyone but you and Tara, so I didn't realize volunteering was an option."

"It absolutely is." Nancy's insides leapt. Since Amelia had been dropped off, she'd acquired more help then she'd ever had. Either the Lord was blessing her in her time of need, or it was connected somehow to Amelia—well, the sweet cherub was the reason Angie thought of it to begin with, so clearly they were connected.

Nancy handed Angie a bookmark with the library's web address printed on it. "There's an online application. Once you fill that out and pass the background check, I'll be in touch about the schedule."

"Sounds easy enough." Angie turned and waved to Lacy, who stood a few feet away, clearly trying to give them privacy while still close enough to hear every word. Angie left the library with the application in hand.

Nancy faced Lacy who stood several feet away. "Thanks for your help today."

"Sure." Lacy's boots clicked on the concrete floor as she walked closer. "You were watching someone's baby here?"

"Sort of. We had a guest last week."

"By guest, do you mean a baby?"

Nancy nodded. "I figured the whole town knew by

now that someone abandoned her baby outside the library last Monday."

"She was abandoned?" Lacy's voice rose. "That's...horrible. What happened to her?"

"Children's protective service came and got her. It's so sad."

"I can't believe anyone would do something like that."

"I know," Nancy said. "It's sad. Are you able to hang out longer?"

Lacy looked at her watch—it was half past one. A worried look filled her eyes. "You didn't get to eat, did you?"

"No. But I can nibble on my sandwich at my desk if you need to take off. I really appreciate you stopping in today. I don't recall what your major is, but I'm looking to hire another assistant. The listing is online if you're interested."

"I might be. With school and stuff, I've been super busy, but I'm thinking of taking next semester off to save up more money and catch my breath."

"That's a good idea, but the position is an immediate opening. I couldn't wait until after Christmas."

Her shoulders drooped slightly. "I understand. I'll think about it anyway. I might be able to make it work, since most of my classes are online."

"I thought all of them were."

"All but two."

Nancy nodded. That made sense since Lacy had come in that one time because her classes had been cancelled.

"I'm still on the schedule for tomorrow, right?"

"Yes. See you."

Lacy grabbed her backpack from under the desk then left, leaving Nancy alone with Angie and with her worries. What if no one applied for the position? She'd be stuck here all the time—she really shouldn't have left Lacy here by herself considering she was only a volunteer, but she was desperate. Speaking of which, the sandwich from Roaster's was calling her.

Adam sat behind his desk at the newspaper office. It had been a painfully slow day. How had Tara spent her day in protective custody with the marshals? Was she bored? Lonely? He'd wanted to stay with her, but in the end the choice had been taken from him, since the marshals wouldn't allow him to accompany her.

He'd learned one important thing in the short time he'd known Tara—she was the real deal. What you saw with her was what you got. She was not fake or phony like Rachel had been. Sure, Tara was reserved and hesitant to let him into her life, but once she had, everything changed. He now realized what he'd felt for Rachel back in college didn't measure up to his feelings for Tara.

He'd loved Rachel, but with Tara it was more than love. There was something about hiding out and running for your life that connected people in a way that he'd never experienced. He missed her, and it hadn't even been a full day since the marshals took over her protection. He prayed it wouldn't be forever, but he had little hope of seeing her again if she went into witness protection. Pain, deep in his being, pulsated. He stood. "I'm going to work from home," he called out to his boss.

"You've been working from home a lot lately." The newspaper's owner stepped out of his office.

"I'm getting my work done," Adam said, his patience wearing thin.

His boss waved a hand. "And it's some of your best work, so I won't stop you but—" he paused and waited until Adam looked at him—"if you ever need someone to talk to, I have my shrink on speed dial."

Adam chuckled dryly. "Thanks." He turned and strode from the building, thankful to be out of there. For a second he thought his boss was going to say he was a good listener—they both knew that'd be a lie.

Adam wandered aimlessly along the main drag. He really didn't want to go home. Maybe a visit with his parents would help his mood. Then again, they'd know immediately that something was up and ask questions he couldn't answer. He found himself standing outside Roaster's Coffee—their "place." The door opened, and two businessmen walked out.

Adam went inside and breathed in deeply of the rich coffee scent. He'd work from here today. He'd missed the lunch rush, so the place was quiet— perfect. "Hi, Pepper. What do you have that will get my creative juices flowing?"

"How about a double-shot Rocket?"

"What's in it?"

"Two shots of espresso, melted chocolate and a dash of cayenne pepper."

"Sounds good. I'll take a large one." He looked at the dessert window. "And one of those pumpkin face cookies too, please."

"You got it. Where's Tara? The two of you have been practically inseparable."

"You exaggerate." He hoped it hadn't been a mistake coming in here. He didn't want to answer questions about Tara.

"It's a gift." Pepper shrugged. "I'll make your drink and bring it over." She handed him the cookie with a piece of tissue-like paper.

"Thanks." He found a corner seat near the window and unlocked his laptop.

The door to the shop opened and Deputy Carter Malone strolled in. He waved to Pepper then headed straight for Adam.

His shoulders tensed. "What's up, Deputy?"

"I saw you from the window and thought I'd check and see how you're doing. I heard about last night from Lyle. Sounds like it was intense."

"It was, but Tara is safe now. In the end, that's all that matters." His conscience ate at him. "Okay, that's a lie. I miss her."

Carter nodded. "I figured as much. You don't get thrust into a situation like that and not develop...feelings."

"It shows?"

"To anyone with eyes."

"I've never have been able to hide my feelings. Sitting in the office is driving me nuts, so I'm heading home to work when I'm done here."

Carter clapped him on the shoulder. "Hang in there. Things are bound to look up soon." He pivoted and left.

"Thanks." He appreciate Carter's attempt to make him feel better, but it didn't help.

Pepper ambled over to his table and placed a large mug on his table. "Let me know what you think."

He picked up the mug, admired the leaf design on the top of the drink then took a careful sip. "It has a kick."

Pepper watched with anticipation on her face.

He sipped again. "The chocolate is smooth. It's a nice combo. A new creation?"

She nodded. "I'm glad you like it. I've been testing it out on customers all week. I think I finally nailed the recipe." She grinned.

"I agree. It's delicious." He raised the cup to her and took another sip. Yep, this was a winner. Now to write an article that would rival the coffee. Inspiration finally struck, and his fingers clicked at the keys.

Chapter Nineteen

NANCY LOCKED UP THE LIBRARY AND walked toward her car. Today had been a long day, and she was thankful it was over. Carter would be at the florist soon. She had plenty of time to meet him. She'd run home first, grab a bite to eat, then head back to their meeting.

Nancy waved to the shopkeeper sweeping the sidewalk in front of his place across the street.

"Nancy! I need to show you something." He motioned her to come over.

She looked both ways then jogged across the road. "What's up, Walt?" The older man wore jeans, a plaid shirt, and work boots.

"Remember that storm we had last Monday?"

"How could I forget?"

"Yeah, it was a strong one. So much so that when it knocked out the power I assumed it killed my security camera too. The thing is, I forgot about something."

A jolt shot through Nancy. "What's that?"

"There's a battery in the camera as a backup for times like that."

"Are you telling me you have footage of that morning?"

A gleam lit his eyes. "Want to see?"

"Lead the way." She restrained herself from dragging the man into the store.

"I have the footage for that morning in my cloud

server. My computer is in the office." He walked past several rows of tools before stopping and unlocking a door. "I keep it locked. You can never be too careful."

"Good thinking." Considering the amount of inventory he had out front, she couldn't imagine what was so valuable in the office that warranted a locked door, but who was she to judge.

He pressed a few keys on the keyboard, and a grainy image pulled up. He pointed. "See there. A woman is standing under the cover in front of the library holding the baby carrier."

"And there's a man over there. I'm surprised she didn't notice him." Nancy leaned in closer to the screen.

"Me too. But look how cagy she is."

"I see." The woman jerked her head side to side. She pulled something from her pocket then slipped it into the diaper bag—probably the note they'd found.

The man approached the woman. He handed her a large envelope, and she handed him the baby carrier. She ran toward the street and jumped into the driver's seat of an old Honda. She pulled away so fast her car fishtailed.

The man pulled what looked to be a bag from a compartment in the carrier. He looked over his shoulder then stuffed it back in the infant seat, tucked Amelia behind the planter beside the doors, and darted out of sight.

Tara ran up the sidewalk and nearly crashed into the automatic doors that didn't open.

Nancy's pulse thrummed in her ears. "She's lucky he didn't confront her."

"What I can't figure out is why he didn't take the

baby with him," Walt said.

"Looks like he panicked. Maybe he thought Tara was someone else."

"Whatever he thought, it probably saved that poor baby." He pointed to the screen. "Keep watching. It gets even more interesting." The library doors slid open, and Tara went inside. "Look there. See that car drive by slowly with the window down only an inch?"

Nancy gasped. "Is that the barrel of a gun?"

"Looks like it to me."

"If Tara had been there even a few seconds longer..." She shivered. "My mom needs to see this right away."

"Will you email it to the sheriff's department?"

"If I knew how." Walt's necked reddened.

"It's fine. I can do it." Her fingers flew across the keys, and a moment later, the file was on its way. "Thanks for showing me this, Walt, but it would be best if you don't mention this to anyone else."

"Don't have to tell me twice. I know trouble when I see it, and that is trouble. I don't know how you managed to keep an abandoned baby out of the gossip chain."

Nancy jogged back to her car and punched the accelerator. This was the break they needed. Too bad the footage was so grainy. It was impossible to see the faces enough to identity the people in the footage, but she had a strong feeling she knew the woman.

Nancy parked in the courthouse parking lot then raced inside and down to the basement where the sheriff's department was located. She flung the door open and went inside.

Everyone stopped what they were doing and

looked her way.

"Sorry. Is Mom in her office?"

A few heads nodded.

She dashed into her mom's office and closed the door. "I sent you an email you're going to want to see."

Her mother frowned. "Nancy, you can't come charging in here like that. You do realize the bullpen has armed deputies?"

She chuckled. "They're not trigger-happy. But I'll try to be more sedate next time. Will you please open your email? I sent you surveillance footage from the morning Amelia was dropped off."

"Where did you get it?" Mom clicked on her computer keyboard.

"Walt, the owner of the shop caddy-corner to the library, thought his camera wasn't working due to the power outage, but then he remembered it had a backup battery." Nancy sat and tapped her heel on the floor, causing her knee to bounce, her mind moving at the speed of light. Her day flashed before her, and she gasped as everything suddenly fell into place. "I know who the baby's mother is."

"You do?" Surprise lit her face. "Is she in the video?"

"No, she's not. Well maybe she is. It's hard to know for sure who the woman with the baby is."

"Then how do you know?"

"The pieces of the puzzle finally fit, but I'm going to need help proving it."

"You got it. Anything you need." Mom frowned as her attention returned to the computer screen. "That car the woman took off in fits the description of car we think hit and killed Rachel Dillon."

Nancy's stomach sickened. As much as she wanted to find Amelia's mother, she desperately hoped she was wrong about the identity of the woman.

Her phone buzzed an incoming text. Carter was at the florist.

"I have to go."

Tara sat holed up in a condo in Bend, Oregon. Two marshals were her 24/7 companions—a male and a female. The female marshal handed her a cup of tea. "Thanks." Tara cradled the cup between her cold hands. She was beginning to think she'd never be warm again.

"We have good news," the female marshal said.

A blip of excitement stirred within her. "What?"

"The timeline for the DEA operation in Florida moved up. They raided the crime syndicate last night at the same time we took your P.I. into custody."

"For real?" Energy surged though her. She set the cup on the coffee table. "Does that mean I'm safe now and can leave?"

She shook her head. "Not yet. The undercover DEA agent will testify against them, but it could take months or even years before this is all over if their attorneys have their way."

"That long?" She hadn't expected the system to move so slowly. Tara titled her head. "I don't have to testify and go into witness protection?"

"Not exactly. They have enough evidence to keep

all of them locked up for a very long time. But there's a good chance someone on the outside is still doing their dirty work. Out of extreme caution, we're providing you with a new identity and strongly advise you to lay low and stay away from Florida."

The happy bubble burst. "I can't go home?"

"To Florida?"

She nodded.

"That would be a bad idea. However, we are confident your P.I. didn't rat out your location to them. We believe you'd be safe to return to Tipton. Word on the street is that he was successful in killing you."

"How? And what's the point of a new identity if I'm going to go back to my last known residence?"

"Good questions," the male marshal said. "We take what we do very seriously and would never intentionally tell you to do something we thought could harm you. Would it be best if you started over someplace else? Yes. Is returning to Tipton going to get you killed? Again, probably not."

"Probably?" Her voice squeaked.

"There are no guarantees in life," he said. "We made sure the person who hired your private investigator received word that you'd been taken care of. But reality is, a bus could hit you tomorrow. Life doesn't come with guarantees."

She frowned. That's how Rachel had died—maybe not by a bus, but still... "I see your point." If she started over someplace else she'd never see Adam again. She didn't want that. How had she fallen for him in less than two weeks? Did he feel the same? "If I go back to Tipton with a different name, people will talk."

"Then use the name Tara. If anyone sees that your identification doesn't match your new legal name, tell them Tara is your nickname."

"Actually, it sort of is. Tara isn't really my name."

He nodded, clearly already privy to that information. "You're legal name is now Taylor King."

"I like that." She grinned. "When can I go back to Tipton?"

"Tomorrow morning. We were only going to tell you this if you decided to return. There has been a development with the child abandonment case and the sheriff would like you to help her out, if you think you're up to it.

"Of course I'll help.

Friday morning Nancy sat in her usual booth across from Pepper. She bit into a chocolate donut then washed it down with a medium-roast brewed coffee. "Perfection, like usual."

"Thanks. So what's the verdict on the cake flavors?"

Nancy gasped, nearly choking. "I'm so sorry. It was such a crazy day. They're still in the fridge at the library."

Pepper shook her head and crossed her arms. "What am I going to do with you? If you don't care about this wedding and reception, how do you expect me to do what you hired me to do?"

"I know. I'm sorry. I'll text Carter right now, and we will do it first thing. I promise." She shot off the text.

"What's really going on, Nancy? I know you get distracted, but you seem more so than usual."

"There's a lot going on at the library lately. I've had several new volunteers to train, I'm"—she lowered her voice and looked around to make sure no one was listening— "consulting with the sheriff's department on a serious matter, and then the harvest festival is coming up, and I've done nothing to prepare, and—"

Pepper waved a hand, silencing her. "I get it, you're overwhelmed right now. We've all been there at times, but you need to prioritize."

"How? Everything is super important."

"Not the harvest festival."

"It's a community event, and I love participating. Besides it's my job to have something there to represent the library. It's a great fundraiser, and the community loves buying used books. It's how we pay for the summer reading program."

"Something has to give. You can't do everything. I'm sure the mayor will understand, given your circumstances."

"Maybe. I haven't even begun to work on the festival yet, and I'm still overwhelmed. Maybe I can get volunteers to run it."

"What else can I do to help?" Pepper asked.

"I don't know. Everything I'm dealing with is stuff I have to do."

"Then I'll be praying for you. If anything changes and you feel like you can let me help, please ask."

"But you're busy too."

"Not so much that I can't spare a couple of hours

for my best friend."

Nancy's throat thickened, humbled by her friend's generosity. She cleared her throat. "Thank you. You're the best."

"I know." Pepper's eyes twinkled with mischief. "Now go taste those cupcakes before you forget about them again."

Nancy stood and saluted her friend. "Yes, ma'am." She chuckled at the look of surprise on Pepper's face. She caught the eye of Lacy, where she sat with her computer at a corner table and waved. "See you later?"

"I'll be there." Lacy smiled then returned her attention to her computer.

Nancy stepped out of the coffee shop into a downpour. She flipped up the hood on her coat and rushed to her car. Carter had replied that he'd be waiting for her. She didn't look forward to tasting the cupcakes this morning after having had a donut— way too much sugar for one day. But she would do it for Pepper. She had to hurry though. Things were about to come to a grand finale with her suspect as the star, and she needed to make sure everything was in place.

Chapter Twenty

CARTER STOOD BESIDE THE LIBRARY DOORS, waiting for Nancy. She ran up the walkway from where she had parked. Rain pelted her face. She rushed toward him and planted a kiss on his cheek.

"As much as I love your kisses, I prefer dry ones. You're soaked."

"What? You didn't need another shower?" Nancy chuckled as she unlocked the doors and re-secured them once they were inside. She shrugged out of her rain jacket then hung it on a hook near her desk.

"You never said why you were late to the florist's last night." Carter took her hand as they walked to the mending room.

She opened its door then flipped on the light. "I know. You were in a rush to get home to Gavin, and I didn't want to keep you or the florist waiting any longer. I had a lot to do last night, so figured it would keep. There was a break in the baby case and possibly the hit and run." She led the way into the room and went directly to the mini-fridge.

He frowned. "I hadn't heard." He leaned against the counter, with his stuffed hands in his jean's pockets.

"That's what happens when you have the day off and your fiancée is stretched too thin to remember to update you."

Cater raised a brow.

"Seriously, I was panicked about being late." She pulled the bag from the fridge and brought it over to him.

"Care to fill me in now?" Carter reached into the bag and pulled out a box. He opened the lid then rubbed his hands together. "These all look good."

"They probably are." She reached for one that said chocolate. Pepper had stuck a toothpick into the top of each one with a tag on it stating the name of the cupcake.

Carter followed her lead. "It's okay."

"I agree, but not wow." She tossed the other half into the garbage.

"What'd you do that for?"

"I'm not going to eat the whole thing." Nancy reached for another mini cupcake.

"I would've finished it for you." He looked longingly toward the garbage can.

"Did you skip breakfast?" She had a suspicion he considered dessert for breakfast acceptable.

"Yes. I was about ready to make something when I got your text."

She grinned. "You can have the rest of what I don't eat, but it's not much of a breakfast."

Five minutes later they'd narrowed it down to their top three favorites. Strawberry, white, and red velvet. Nancy started a pot of coffee. "I'm in sugar overload." She wrapped an arm across her upset belly.

Carter popped one of Nancy's leftovers into his mouth. "Not me. You were going to tell me about the break in the case."

"I never said that." She shot him a silly grin. "But

because I love you, I'll share." She told him about the video and her suspect and what she had planned for later.

Carter pulled her to him. "I'm proud of you, Nancy. But I'm also concerned. What if your suspect gets violent?"

"She won't."

"You can't be sure. People are unpredictable."

"Not all people. She's not a hardened criminal."

"You don't know that." His eyes pleaded with her to be careful.

"You're right, but my gut says she's not going to hurt me."

"I think I'll spend my day off in the library today."

"That's not necessary." She loved him for his overprotectiveness. Surprise hit her—that trait used to annoy her. When had things changed?

"I know. But it'll be fun. I'll even get take-out for us at lunch time."

"Well, when you put it like that, I can't say no." She kissed him again.

His arms tightened around her, and he drew her closer, deepening the kiss until tingles zipped through her. After a moment he released her. "Our wedding day is too far away."

"We can always elope." She winked.

He chuckled. "I should've known you'd say that."

She poured them each a cup of coffee and handed one to him. He wrinkled his nose. "You have any sugar or cream?"

"Nope. You have plenty of sugar and cream in you already."

He laughed. "I prefer them together, not in

courses.”

She chuckled. “I need to get busy. You’re welcome to hang out in here or find a comfy chair in the reading area.” She left without looking back because if she did, she was liable to end up back in his arms and not accomplish anything before the library opened.

Several hours later Nancy glanced at the clock for probably the fiftieth time since starting work. The day had dragged as soon as she’d opened the doors. Carter sat in the reading area, seemingly engrossed in a novel, but she knew he was very much aware of anything and everything going on around him.

The doors slid open. Show time.

Tara carried baby Amelia into the library. Sheriff Daley had coordinated with the marshals and children’s protective services to have her bring the baby into the library. She was told to say she was watching Amelia for a friend and to follow Nancy’s lead. She’d tried to get them to tell her more, but they wouldn’t. However, she had a pretty good guess—Nancy was up to something and had the full support of the law behind her.

Nancy’s face broke into a wide grin. She spoke quietly to the blonde-haired woman sitting beside her then stood. “Welcome back. You brought a friend?”

“The daughter of a friend. This is Amelia.”

“We’ve met,” Nancy cooed as she placed her finger into the baby’s grip. Amelia stared up at her with blue eyes.

"Amelia?" The blonde woman croaked.

"Oh, I'm sorry. I forgot you don't know Tara. Lacy, this is Tara, my librarian assistant, and sweet Amelia."

Lacy's face had turned sheet white. "This is your *friend's* daughter?" Her gaze was trained on the baby.

"Yes. She asked me to watch her for a couple of hours," Tara said. "Isn't she adorable? Would you like to hold her?"

Nancy shot her an are-you-crazy look.

"I um...are you sure her mom wouldn't mind?" Lacy asked.

"I don't see why she would." Tara placed the carrier on the desktop and unstrapped the precious bundle then gently passed her over to Lacy.

Lacy stared at the carrier for a moment as she cradled Amelia in her arms until the infant reached up and grasped her hair. Her gaze transferred to Amelia. She gently disentangled her hair from the baby's grasp. She cradled the infant as if she was the most precious gift ever. Her eyes glistened. "I never thought I'd see you again," she said softly.

Tara's gaze shot to Nancy's.

Nancy shook her head and eased down to sit beside Lacy again. "Do you know Amelia?"

Lacy nodded and stroked Amelia's fuzzy head. "She's...my...daughter."

Nancy rubbed her back. "How is it you don't have her anymore?"

Tears rolled down her face, and Tara blinked back a few of her own. Clearly, Lacy loved her daughter, so why did she abandon her?

"I needed money. I lost my job."

"You had a job?" Nancy asked.

"Yes. I worked at a bank, but then I had problems with my pregnancy and missed a lot of work."

"They can't fire you for that," Nancy said.

"I'd only worked there a short while—long enough to have health insurance, but not long enough to have a bunch of paid time off. When my vacation time and sick leave ran out, and I didn't show up to work after a week, I received a call informing me I was fired."

"But Oregon has protected maternity leave. They weren't allowed to fire you." Nancy didn't hide her anger. "They can't get away with that."

"They didn't know," Lacy said softly while gazing at her daughter. "I hide my pregnancy. I was afraid they wouldn't hire me if they knew I was pregnant and then once I started there, I was afraid I wouldn't get past my trial period if they found out."

"But you lost your job anyway." Tara hurt for this woman. She had been through a lot. But still the choices she'd made were terrible. "I don't know how they couldn't know you were pregnant."

Lacy stroked Amelia's cheek. "I carried her more toward my back than my front and didn't show much. Plus she was so tiny—only six pounds. I couldn't afford to pay for gap insurance, but since I'd had insurance when I registered and paid for school, I received an exemption for having to purchase it. The bills were piling up. I didn't know what else to do. I'd already paid for my fall semester tuition, and it was past the date to get my money back. My rent was due, and I didn't have any place to live except my car." She sobbed.

Amelia burst into tears. Nancy gently took her from Lacy and cradled the infant to her chest. She stood and bounced her gently until her wails silenced. "Why did you enroll in school when you knew you'd have Amelia?"

"I'm mostly taking online classes. I only have one morning of classes, and I figured I'd hire a sitter for that day. I don't have family in the area and even if I did they wouldn't help me."

Sheriff Daley stepped out from behind nearby stacks. "Spoken like a woman who has no clue how much work a baby is. Sleepless nights and endless crying."

Lacy jumped and wiped her face with the back of her hand. "It was horrible. I wanted to be a good mom, but I wasn't. I tried." Her pleading eyes took in all three women. "I really tried to do it all by myself, but it was too much."

"So what did you do?" Sheriff Daley asked.

"I heard about someone who would pay cash for babies. I talked to him, and he said the babies are placed in the homes of wealthy people who haven't been able to have children of their own. He said she'd be well cared for and loved. I don't understand how she ended up here. I figured a family outside of the area would adopt her. I was so upset that day. I took the money and just drove. The rain pelted my car. Between that, the fog, and my tears, it was almost impossible to see. It was the worst day of my life."

"Is that your white Honda in the parking lot?"

Lacy nodded.

"Are you aware of the front end damage on it?" sheriff Daley asked.

"Yes. I hit something in the fog that day. I think maybe a deer or a small tree. I don't know. I never saw it. I don't have money to get my car fixed."

Sheriff Daley's brows drew together. "Lacy, you're under arrest for vehicular manslaughter and child trafficking."

Her jaw dropped. "I didn't kill anyone, and I didn't traffic any children."

The sheriff cuffed her hands behind her back. "Selling a baby, even your own, is against the law."

"I didn't know." Panic filled her voice. "Honest. And I didn't kill anyone."

"We have probable cause to believe your car was involved in the death of Rachel Dillon."

"What are you talking about?" Tears streamed down Lacy's face.

"Didn't you hear about the woman who was hit by a car and left for dead that same day?" Nancy asked.

"Oh, no. Are you saying that I...?" Her eyes pleaded with them to believe her. "I didn't know. I've been too busy with school and stuff to pay attention to the news."

Compassion mixed with anger toward this woman. How could one person be so clueless and mess up so badly? Tara shook her head. She'd give about anything to have a sweet angle like Amelia for a daughter, but Lacy sold her.

"Let's go." Sheriff Daley hauled Lacy out the door.

Carter stepped over to them. "That was quite a show."

"Thanks for making sure everyone got out before Tara arrived," Nancy said.

Tara looked around. "I didn't realize we were alone."

"Mom was afraid if it was busy when you walked in, Lacy wouldn't open up."

"I think she was right," Carter said.

"It's so sad." Tara reached out for Amelia. "To have such a gift and to give her up."

"Desperate people do desperate things." Carter sat beside Nancy and took her hand.

Tara's heart squeezed. She missed Adam.

The marshals came out of hiding and walked over to Tara. "We need to be going. It would be best if you lay low for a few months, but it's up to you."

Tara nodded. "Thank you for everything. Please tell the men who rescued me thanks too. I think I forgot. I can't tell you how much I appreciate all the marshals have done. Do you think it will be okay if I call my family?" She'd asked before but hoped things had changed since last night.

"Not yet. Give it until after the trial. Even though you don't have to testify it'd be best to let things simmer down," the female marshal said.

They didn't say no indefinitely. Overcome with relief and gratitude, Tara couldn't find her voice. She blinked back tears and shook each of their hands.

Amelia cooed, breaking the tension.

Tara grinned. "What's going to happen to this sweet girl?"

Carter shook his head. "It's up to a judge to decide."

Tara glanced toward the doors then back at Nancy. "We need to talk, but right now I want to find

Adam. Will you make sure Amelia gets returned to her social worker? She's outside with the marshals."

"Absolutely." Nancy took the baby from her and placed her in the carrier.

"Adam said something about working from home," Carter said.

"Thanks." She couldn't wait to tell him the good news.

Chapter Twenty-One

A FIRM KNOCK ON ADAM'S FRONT door drew his attention. He stood. "Who can that be?" He looked through the peephole, and a jolt of excitement hit him. "Tara." He yanked open the door. "What are you doing here?" He pulled her inside and looked around to make sure no one was watching.

"Relax. The marshals said I'm fine to be in town, but I need to lay low until after the trial."

"You're not going to testify? Not going into witness protection?" He didn't know how to feel. On one hand, he was thrilled she wasn't lost to him forever. But on the other, he was scared for her. What if they found her again?

"No. I'm not. The undercover agent is going to testify. The people who ordered me killed were informed that I'm dead. I have a new identity, and I'm supposed to lay low for a few months. I was wondering if you'd like to take that island vacation we talked about?"

"Just like that? Leave?"

"Why not? You can write from anywhere?"

"Well, not exactly, if I'm employed by the Tipton paper. I can't report local news from an island in the Caribbean."

"So freelance. Write a book. Take pictures and put them in a book. Write for a travel magazine. I need to lay low for a long while. Maybe a couple of years."

He touched a finger to her lips. "I get it. I'd love to go with you but only under one condition."

"Anything."

He dropped to one knee.

She gasped and covered her mouth with her hands. "What are you doing?"

"Tara."

"Taylor."

"Excuse me?"

"Technically my name is Taylor now."

"Is that what you want me to call you?"

"I kind of like it. Tara is my middle name, and I was never terribly fond of it."

"Okay, but it's going to take some getting used to. Don't get mad if I slip up now and then."

"I promise."

He cleared his throat. "Taylor, my world turned upside down the day I met you. You are both exhilarating and frustrating."

"Uh."

He chuckled. "Let me finish. As I was saying. You make sure life is anything but boring, and you bring out the best in me. I love you. Will you marry me?"

"Yes. I love too. But don't you think we're rushing things?"

"When it's right, you know in here." He touched a hand to his heart and stood. "And it's right."

Her eyes twinkled. "I agree." She wrapped her arms around his neck.

"I like that sound of those words on your lips." He captured her mouth with his and kissed her silly.

She pulled away. "We need to stop kissing and get

down to the courthouse to apply for our marriage license.”

“Good idea. I want to marry you as soon as possible so we can get you out of here safe and sound. I know the marshals said you’re safe here, but I’d feel better being far, far away.”

“You sure you know what you’re getting yourself into?”

“Do you have any more secrets?”

She shook her head. “Only that I think you are the most amazing man I’ve ever known, and I feel like the most blessed woman ever.”

His face heated. “Clearly you’re biased. After we apply for our marriage license, I want you to meet my family.” He couldn’t wait to introduce Tara or rather Taylor to his parents. They were going to love her. He shot off a text to his mom to let her know to expect a special guest for dinner tonight.

Something niggled at the back of Nancy’s mind. Why did it feel like she was missing something? All the bad guys were in custody. Tara was safe, Lacy, though a sad situation, would be held accountable for her actions—so why did she feel this way?

She flicked a pencil between her fingers and ambled through the stacks in the library. Carter had effectively kicked everyone out and no one had come in since. Word must have traveled that something was going on here. She was glad because the quiet gave her thinking time.

She thought back to when Tara had come in with

Amelia. Lacy had been shocked to her core to find out her baby was still in town. But something was off.

Her eyes widened. "Oh my goodness! The drugs." She sent Carter a text telling him to meet her at the sheriff's department. She had a hunch. She grabbed her stuff then quickly locked up. It was early, and she was liable to get an earful from the mayor but this was too important to wait.

She hopped into her Mustang and floored the gas. Her tires squealed as she pulled away from the curb. A few minutes later she jogged into the courthouse and trotted down the stairs to the basement.

Carter stood outside the department entrance waiting for her.

"You got here fast." She strode toward him.

"I was already here. What's your excuse?"

"Lead foot."

He chuckled and opened the door for her. "You mom is observing Lacy's interrogation."

"I need to talk to her."

"Okay. Hold on." He spoke to Lyle.

Lyle glanced her way with a frown and shook his head.

"Not this time." She walked up to him. "Lyle, have I asked to do anything like this before?"

"Not exactly."

Maybe she had, but she sure didn't remember it. "Do you think I would ask if it wasn't important?"

"I suppose not. But this goes against protocol."

She raised a brow. "I'm the one who cracked this case wide open. Now please let me wrap it up."

Both men stared at her with curiosity.

"I say we let her," Carter said.

"Really?" Lyle rubbed his chin. "Okay. You know where to go."

"Thanks." Adrenaline flooded Nancy's veins. She hustled to the viewing room and went inside.

Her mom did a double-take. "What are you doing in here?" she said softly.

"Something was eating at me. Has anyone asked her about the drugs in Amelia's carrier?"

"Not yet."

"I think she put them there." She pointed toward Lacy who sat at a table on the other side of the mirrored window. "Did you see how her gaze locked onto the carrier when Tara handed her Amelia? It was only when her daughter yanked on her hair that she stopped staring at it."

"Do you think she was dealing?"

"I don't know, but I'd like to find out."

"That would explain why we couldn't figure out the drug angle. Okay. Stay here." Her mom left the room, and a moment later she entered the interrogation room and sat beside the deputy questioning, Lacy. "New evidence has been brought to my attention."

Lacy looked wary.

"There were drugs found in your daughter's baby carrier. How did they get there?"

"I don't know."

"You're in enough trouble as it is, don't make it harder on yourself by lying. Tell us who your supplier is, and I'll put in a good word for you with the District Attorney."

Lacy's eyelids closed. She bit down on her bottom lip. After a moment she opened them. "Fine.

Everything I said at the library was true, but I left out the drug part. The person I'd contacted about Amelia told me he'd throw in some extra cash if I would deliver a package for him too. I didn't know it was drugs at first."

"So the man you delivered your baby to was not the same person you spoke with to set up the exchange."

"Correct. I know it was wrong, but I needed the money. It was a one-time deal. Then the guy came back to me the next day. He said the package hadn't been delivered, and I was responsible."

"What'd you do?" The deputy leaned toward her.

"At first, I wasn't sure what to do, but the more I thought about it, the more I was convinced the package must have fallen out somewhere on the library grounds. I figured if anyone had found it, Nancy would know. So I came up with a plan to volunteer at the library. I'd get Nancy to trust me, and then I'd ask if she'd found anything unusual."

"Did you ask her?" the deputy asked.

"No. I never had the chance. Ironically, I was going to today. The man was growing impatient, and I was scared he would follow through with his threat."

"Which was," Nancy's mom asked.

"He said he'd kill my daughter."

"What's the man's name?"

"I called him Mr. Smith."

"Probably an alias," the deputy said. "Could you describe him to a sketch artist?"

"I think so."

Nancy's mom stood. "I'll get it set up. Thank you, Lacy. I'll hold up my end of the bargain if you hold up yours."

"I will." Lacy looked like she'd aged ten years in the past hour. Nancy felt for her, but at the same time it was difficult to feel too much compassion after what she'd done. She left the viewing room and met her mom in the hall.

"Well done. You managed to not only solve the baby case, but you wrapped up the drug case as well as the hit and run. You sure you don't want to become a cop? You're getting pretty good at this."

Nancy shook her head. "Thanks, but no thanks."

Her mom grinned. "Somehow I knew you'd say that."

Nancy found Carter in the bullpen and told him everything.

"You're one amazing woman." He kissed her there in front of everyone. Her face flamed. "Sorry. I know you don't like public displays of affection."

"I could get used to them."

He tossed his head back and laughed. "Let's get out of here."

Epilogue

Christmas Eve

NANCY STOOD JUST INSIDE THE LIBRARY doors with her arm looped through Lyle's. A long white "carpet" stretched from her toes to the center of the open space in front of the circulation desk where an arch-shaped arbor stood decorated in little white lights, pinecones, greenery and red poinsettia flowers. Six rows of five chairs flanked each side of the carpet. Small sprays with pinecones and greenery with white poinsettias were attached to the end chair at each of the six rows.

Lyle patted her hand. "You're nervous."

"How'd you know?"

"You're gripping my arm like your life depends on it."

"Oh. Sorry." She relaxed her hand. "It's really something, isn't it? I never imagined my wedding would turn out so well." She took in the sight before her. They'd managed to turn the library into a legit wedding venue.

"From what I've heard, you have Carter to thank for that."

"He was insistent on doing this wedding right. So yeah, pretty much. He's amazing." He'd taken over the wedding preparations since she'd been swamped at the library. With Tara and Adam off on an extended honeymoon to a super-secret location, she had to hire a new library assistant. Which meant training and long hours. She still couldn't believe they eloped. At least she'd been able to attend their wedding as one of their witnesses.

Carter had made sure everything turned out perfectly, right down to the five-piece instrumental ensemble squeezed into a corner to the right of the arbor. She looked down at her white, twenties-inspired tea-length dress. Even though she hadn't cared much about the wedding to begin with, she had considered what she'd wear and knew exactly what she'd wanted.

The ensemble began playing Pachelbel's "Cannon in D."

"Here we go," Lyle said.

Nancy smiled. "Maybe someday that will be you standing up front waiting for your bride."

"I know you think your mom and I belong together, but we have a good thing going. I don't want to mess that up."

Nancy patted his hand. "Whatever you say, Lyle." She stepped forward. Pepper met her gaze and gave her a thumbs-up. Nancy laughed. Mom waited at the front row of chairs, wearing a purple pantsuit. Carter stood beside their pastor looking handsome in a black tux. His eyes sparkled as he grinned. His nephew, Gavin, was his best man and looked almost as handsome as his uncle.

Carter's gaze locked onto hers and didn't let go. Her heart raced in anticipation of their future. The music silenced when she stopped at the arbor. Pepper gave her a thumbs up, and Anna looked radiant in a plum, knee-length-dress. If things continued as they were, Nancy guessed the next wedding she'd be attending would be Anna and Luke's.

Pastor Davis addressed their guests then turned his focus to them. Nancy's heart pounded. She'd hardly slept last night thanks to her nerves. How did people do this? The pastor prompted them in their vows and before it seemed possible he pronounced them husband and wife.

"Carter, you may kiss your bride," Pastor Davis said.

With one arm over her shoulder and one around her waist, Carter dipped her back and planted a toe-tingling kiss on her lips. Their guests clapped and whistled, and she didn't even care. She kissed Carter back with more fervor than she realized she possessed. He raised her upright and their lips parted.

"Sweet junipers," Nancy said.

"You can say that again." Carter grinned.

They turned and marched hand in hand with their guests following, from the library to Roaster's Coffee. "We did it," Nancy said.

"When I moved to Tipton a little more than a year ago and arrested you for trespassing, I never imagined I'd marry you."

Nancy laughed.

"You laugh now. But no one was laughing then," Carter said.

"That's for sure. I was so miffed with you. I still can't believe you arrested me."

"I still can't believe you broke a window to get into a house for cupcakes."

"It was an emergency. Are we really going to rehash this on our wedding day?" She raised a brow.

"Nope. In fact, I solemnly promise to never mention it again."

"Good. Same with me."

He held the door open at Roaster's for her. "After you."

She dipped her chin and strode into a wonderland. "This can't be the coffee shop." Snowflakes with twinkle lights hung from the ceiling. Every table was covered with a white linin tablecloth. Some kind of purple flower filled a clear glass vase at each table. "It's stunning."

Pepper charged out from the kitchen—she must have run here and then entered from the backdoor. "What do you think?" She opened her arms.

"You went above and beyond." Nancy rushed to her and gave her a hug. "Thank you! It's beautiful."

"I'm glad you like it. It's my gift to you." Pepper's voice cracked.

"Now don't start with that, or you'll make me cry, and I'm an ugly crier."

Pepper chuckled. "Sorry. We can't have the bride looking ugly. I have a spot reserved for you and Carter at this table." She pulled her over to a corner of the room where a long skinny metal stand said "bride, groom" and "wedding party."

"It's perfect. I hope you'll be able to have some fun too and not be working the entire time."

"I will. My work here is finished, unless there's a crisis. I hired a couple of students to stand beside the dessert tables and take care of your guests."

"Good. You're the best, Pepper. One day, when

you get married, I want to be there for you like you have been for me."

"I'll hold you to that."

Nancy hugged her one more time before moving to Carter's side to greet their guests as they filed in. She spoke into his ear. "You were right."

"About what?"

"This. Having a wedding rather than eloping was a great idea. Think of everything we would've missed if we'd eloped."

"Exactly." He placed a soft kiss on her forehead. "I love you."

"I love you more."

Author Note

Tipton is a fictional town placed in the Willamette Valley near Salem. I love setting stories in fictional small towns because it gives me creative license to do anything I want. I hope you enjoyed the result.

For those of you who enjoy real life locations, the county courthouse in Dallas, Oregon inspired the Tipton county courthouse.

If you enjoyed this book, I'd love if you'd be willing to leave a review on any of your favorite book sites, like ChristianBook.com, Amazon.com, Goodreads.com, BarnesandNoble.com or others. It's such a help to an author when reviews are posted. Here are a few places you can connect with me:

Subscribe to Kimberly's newsletter to learn about upcoming releases, sales, and to simply stay in contact:
www.kimberlyrjohnson.com
Join Kimberly on Facebook:
www.facebook.com/KimberlyRoseJohnson
Follow Kimberly on Amazon: http://amzn.to/2jArIFU
Follow Kimberly on BookBub:
www.bookbub.com/authors/kimberly-rose-johnson
Follow Kimberly on Instagram:
www.instagram.com/kimberlyrosejohnsonauthor/

Books by Kimberly Rose Johnson

Brides of Seattle
The Reluctant Groom

Melodies of Love
A Love Song for Kayla
An Encore for Estelle
A Waltz for Amber

Sunriver Dreams
A Love to Treasure
A Christmas Homecoming
Designing Love

Wildflower B&B Romance Series
Island Refuge
Island Dreams
Island Christmas
Island Hope

Contemporary Inspirational Romance Collection
In Love and War

Contemporary Novella
Brewed with Love

www.ingramcontent.com/pod-product-compliance
Lightning Source LLC
Chambersburg PA
CBHW070638170726
48291CB00003B/1060